# MY PRECIOUS

# MY PRECIOUS

MELISSA JOANE CHÂTEL

RESOURCE *Publications* · Eugene, Oregon

MY PRECIOUS

Resource Publications
An Imprint of Wipf and Stock Publishers
199 W. 8th Ave., Suite 3
Eugene, OR 97401

www.wipfandstock.com

PAPERBACK ISBN: 978-1-4982-8283-3
HARDCOVER ISBN: 978-1-4982-8284-0
EBOOK ISBN: 978-1-4982-8285-7

Manufactured in the U.S.A.                                        01/03/19

# Contents

# Diary of Melissa Joane Châtel 5
## Written November 30, 2014 . . .

I WOULD LIKE TO thank a few people who made sure that my dream came true. I believe that, without them, I never could have completed what I now know I was born to do. This true passion left me unsatisfied at certain times in my life and without explanation when I saw that I was not doing what I needed to fill that void. To my mother who, despite her lack of education, attended to mine in the most extraordinary way: Loude Saint-Jean Châtel. To my three little sisters: Jenny Châtel, Lindsay Dafka Fleurilus Châtel and Deborah Fabianie Fleurilus Châtel. To my two older brothers who are always in my thoughts: Jimmy Patric Châtel, Jhonny Châtel. To my sister-in-law and best friend as well as her mother: Kassandre Carrara, Gladis Lopez. My older brother: Achile Châtel. To my best friend: Sandra Simas. To my other best friend: Rabia Mir To: François Rainville. To the love of my life: Sylvain Lachaine. To my long-time friend, who has become like a father to me: Lucien A. Levac. Even if you do not appear in this story for a million reasons, I want to tell you it's you who will look after all my finances. To Bernard Gobin, once again, for his valuable time and his assistance. To my first publishing house, Vérone, for everything. To: David Koch. To: Antonio Raphael. To one of my good friend: Zak Santiago. To: Nick Cadarelli.

To the rest of my family and close friends for their support and their understanding. Thank you again with all my heart.

# *Etener*

LIFE IS AN ETERNAL battle between good and evil that man called "Etener." Man claims that to prevail, we must know the laws of "Etener" and be prepared to overcome it with the right weapons.

Only at the end of the Ying and Yang battle the winner can be determined: You or life.

## *Châtel's Theory*

There will always be matter that mankind may never comprehend. Most of it is already gone, but we are, however, aware of their previous existences. The rest is simple, even if it is not visible, it permanently remains in the atmosphere.

Nevertheless, for the very few who come to experience or even feel its existence , their lives has been transformed and changed forever; making them stand out from most people.

The visible world that we live in became our reality there exists, in parallel with our world, another creation that is much more advanced than ours. Those who are aware of this and know about its existence have long called it "the invisible world." We are now aware that everything that exists in our world has already existed in the other because they are light years ahead of us. This world's greatest creations come from them; they watch everything and carefully influence the right creator. In truth, a question always comes to mind each time I think about it: Why do all intellects throughout time say that before founding a great idea, they felt a kind of energy, which was then followed by the emergence of their creation? Today, we know that the influencers appear in various ways and take forms that you would perhaps never imagine.

To follow up on what was mentioned in my first book, "The legend of the sisters souls" on how the world had been created according to our primary thoughts is a minor matter compared to what will follow when I share with the happenings to come, still based on our intuitions.

This book, my second and as Precious as the long list of the memorable books you will be able to read through the course of time, will make you smile, cry and talk about me—saying good or perhaps even bad things about me. I won't blame you, but I can assure you that what I was yesterday and the burdensome past that I lived through have made me the wonderful woman I am today. Learn from me and you will also be able to successfully find your way through life.

I perhaps should have started with an introduction that would allow you to get to know me better, but have chosen not to do that. I am different from many writers you usually read, but you will never learn as much from them as you will from me. I will surprise you in a remarkable way by sharing my world among some real and fictional characters, some of whom already exist in this world and have never been seen by a son of Adam.

Before beginning this story, you should know that even though I had dreamed of this day since I was seven, now that I have finally climbed to the most influential social class in the world, I care very little about it. My name has long since made itself known. Melissa Joane Châtel was synonymous with success from any point of view. And we all know that success has always ruled the world. However the war had taken everything from me, and nothing could change that. To further enlighten you, I should tell you that my other books have all been much more imaginative than this one because it is written with just one goal: to know myself better. I can assure you that everything that I had hoped for throughout my entire life and more really happened. I have seen many years pass that brought me their share of joy. But at the same time and more commonly, I have known sadness. I've come a long way shedding tears, but do not regret this because, in the end, my tears have taught me life lessons and made me stronger.

# CHAPTER 1

# *The Change*

THE CHIN LEE SYSTEM was the key name given to the new faultless inventions designed after World War III. I will not immediately talk about the entire war, which was caused by human vanity and exterminated half the world. But for now, you should know that, on April 28th, 2025, Wold War III broke out. With Russia, Japan, Germany and North Korea in opposition to the United States of America (whose allies were Canada, England and several European countries). At the end of this universal tragedy, the Russian president Coscovi, had gained some allies such as Cuba, Bolivia, Brazil, East Asia and Mexico. They were the first five on a long list of countries that pledged allegiance to Russia that had weapons that was used to annihilate parts of the Earth, these countries were destroyed before the alliance could grow.

Many years ago, Albert Einstein said, "I know not with what weapons World War III will be fought, but World War IV will be fought with sticks and stones." Centuries before that and shortly before his death, Jesus of Nazareth prophesied, "For then shall be great tribulation, such as was not since the beginning of the world to this time, no, nor ever shall be. And except those days should be shortened, there should no flesh be saved: but for the elect's sake those days shall be shortened." (Matthew 24:21–22)

Until the end of time, there will be words that will never fade, an apothegm that you might have heard before "The reason of the strongest is always the best" but is now interpreted differently as has become the basis of our new world .Only the strong could survive in the Chin Lee system of the new century . . .

To understand my world, you need to know since its establishment, the basis of all great success is the mere fact that you and only you can step out of the ordinary, and that if you have the courage, you can make a difference to all those who have lost hope and light. They say, "Only those who believe will actually see the power appear." However, most of these miracles will happen for all those who will make this one difference, whether good or bad, regardless of the world you belong to and regardless of whether you are insignificant or even very great.

My intellect and knowledge are based on my indestructible faith in the universe that has become my raison d'être. As I was progressively evolving in a world like ours, I discovered our many differences and prejudices were linked to race and religion. Our lack of love for those who do not benefit us had in a certain sense provoked all our conflicts and created a world full of demons that were ready to devour the sons of the Earth in one bite.

The result will show you the effort that it took to build my world from absolutely nothing. I have only harvested the fruit of special labours, originating in a perfect harmony that absolutely had to be created and acknowledged throughout the world. Thanks to my perseverance, I earned the favour of my heavenly father, who lives in me as I live in him. Today, the glory that I gain thanks to him makes my works indestructible. The good that I have made out of nothing, and the assistance provided during the war, helped me gain access to the garden that the whole Earth never thought they would one day ever see. All this took some time, but it was necessary. Many have left and did not gain access to it, but the hundreds who held on to hope entered with us. There were guardians responsible for our protection, elected representatives who would define our goal after the chaos of the world and, of course, the saints of the Earth; even though, among the saints, many had fallen and had turned away from the light.

The first of the elect chosen from among the billions worldwide was named Dimitrova Maxalli. He grew up in an orphanage in Russia; however, he came from a long line of Jews of whom he alone was still alive. He was a man of integrity in the eyes of God and had a dream at the end of the fourth year of war, which would become the answer to thousands of the guardians' heartfelt prayers and the saints' refusal to give up. He discovered the gate to the garden of Eden, which had disappeared until that day because of the sins of man. The creator ordered to let two seraphim stay there so that no one could enter. During all this time, the gate was inside a waterfall in the Himalayas, but entry could not be gained without the presence of Dimitrova. In other words, it was the key to the mystery of Etener. We come to the Earth with a specific goal related to the mystery of the end, no matter what this goal is for all of us. For this reason, I would advise each of you to seize even the smallest opportunity to forge ahead because one thing is certain: nothing ventured, nothing gained.

As for me, I just decided, one day in December 2014, to fulfill a promise and become a better person than the one I once was. Although this may seem nonsensical to some of you to believe it, you should know that I trusted in the simple thought that I was no longer alone. I believed it and I still believe it, and one thing is certain because I tell you the truth that everything works toward the good of those who love doing good.

I was born in a country where insecurity and poverty at that time were at their height. I was part of two very different worlds and today I have won the most beautiful victory because I know that one couldn't exist without teaching me a life lesson that would change my view of things while protecting me from the other one that could have simply destroyed me if I hadn't been prepared for such glory. I had somehow been able to build, during the years before the war, the foundations of a future based on concentration; and the results I was getting were what propelled me into the mystery of what was waiting to be discovered years later. As some of you have always known, but others will only later see throughout the passages written inside the oldest book in the world, the Holy Bible. This book alone holds the key to the success of each of us. It had become my strength because I knew the truth about him, and for this reason, he allowed me to pass through all the other doors of this future that you cannot yet understand.

I found my purpose after twenty-six years of questioning, and I pursued it without even wondering whether it would lead to anything. The answer is in us: we know the path and the most difficult part is to take it before it's too late. The only problem that could become an obstacle is placing limits on ourselves. The goal is to think big because you can't go halfway, which is the defect of all major systems in this world.

Today, I am 105 years old. I have finally entered the most influential social class in the world. My name was synonymous with success, and we both know that power has always ruled the world. Right now, I am in one of the most luxurious chalets between heaven and Earth, right above the former Dubai. Considering my age, you can easily think that I'm an old woman walking with a cane, waiting for my grandchildren to visit. Let me enlighten you. What you don't know is that the world had changed. Many malcontents proclaimed far and wide in the beginning that the system was not reliable. Personally, the system had not affected me in any case because I paid a heavy price.

Based on the evolution of the future, we tried to create our own gods . . . Every time, it brought us back to the same starting point, as if we were ignoring something in the information that we had received from the very beginning to transform it and then change the meaning to our own advantage. Science had eventually turned us into true robots, and men built weapons powerful enough to reduce themselves to nothingness. Not even once, during all these years of war, was man able to wonder how it feels for he who created the Earth while leaving us the privilege to rule there.

Of course, like most stories that end well, mine ends in mysterious ways and began in the most ordinary way on earth. As strange as it may seem, I am only going to start toward the end of the story, with the journey, to enable you to better understand the story of my life.

It was in this way the long journey to the promised land began . . .

The war broke out, and things went from bad to worse. All we were able to do was pray because, despite all the money we had, it did not prevent us from feeling that the end was near. We had departed from one of Canada's coasts from a place named Percé not long after the war, the only place in North America that had become, among all the other parts of the world, the safest. We formed a group of over 800 people. My family, Jack's family, most of my close friends from all over and various ministers from many churches across the world, or at least all the ones who were able to join us not long after and whose presence was a blessing for all of us. All my best friends who had listened to me and followed were there with us; many other people that I didn't know were also there. One day, before I realized it, the Apostle Isaac, his family and other close friends came to join us again. He was the man who had largely directed my spiritual life and made me into a better person. He was also the one who had married me to Jack. I was very happy to see them arrive. It was rumoured that Mr. Obama had arrived a month earlier, but I had not yet come across him. I was quite curious to know why he was here and not elsewhere. It had been two years since anyone had seen the former head of state, and this was becoming very strange. I had a thousand questions to ask him, but I had to wait for the right moment because, according to the others, he was always busy and never seemed very willing to engage in conversation.

The first years of war destroyed Japan, Brazil and East Asia and, as expected, my little sister Déborah gave birth to a little boy, who was named Jacob. He represented hope when compared to all the lives that had left the earth since the beginning of the war. We continued to pray, asking for the grace of God in the face of all those demonic spirits who wanted to see us wipe ourselves out across the planet. Quietly, they had allowed us to destroy each other, and their work would not stop until we all disappeared. But some good people remained who still wanted to worship and give glory to God, even with the chaos that reigned. We still followed the principles and the word despite everything. Americans had occupied a major part of Canadian territory for over a year. They felt no shame in recruiting all the adolescents they found along the way on the battlefields of the war. Florida was devastated and half of the world was destroyed at the beginning of the fourth year of a war that seemed like it would never stop. Europe had not responded for a year, and the damage was even more catastrophic there than elsewhere. "The Titan" was the name they gave this struggle to which nobody seemed to see an end. We were running out of food, and we were worried about our lives and imagined that the worst was yet to come. We held on to the hope that God could not abandon us, and we only prayed all the more fervently that he provide respite for us, the victims of this abomination.

Winter was rapidly approaching that year and, for the first time in the history of the world, the climate did not change and remained as if we were still in springtime. It was one of those miracles that we would never be able to forget and that played a significant role in our survival. At the same time, two weeks later, it was a disaster when we watched several American ships land on Percé's coastline. We were afraid that another part of Canada would again find itself under siege and occupied. They kept saying on the air since their arrival that it was only for security reasons. A month after their appearance in the ports, Dimitrova had a dream that confirmed what we had known for a long time. He saw only twelve of us leaving Percé to undertake a very long journey. These twelve would cross the entire Atlantic in order to find the passage that would allow the other elect of the Earth to live. This war would destroy the Earth, leaving behind a frail, devastated surface with no life. He didn't tell any of us about the dream until he had it more than once; we saw that he no longer was at peace with himself. I trusted my instinct because I had long ago understood how he did things. I decided to go ask him about his sudden change in mood because, before I took the initiative, no one had really dared to do so. Eventually, after an interminable hour of questioning, he told me about his dream, which, as I listened to it, seemed crazier than ever.

"Only twelve of us? I asked him with a hushed, small voice once he had confessed his fears to me.

—" And my wife," he said, for fear of losing her. "She will be with me for the trip, and I could see every other person that would come with us, Mel. I can guarantee you that this will not be a yearlong trip but one that will last six years. I would just like to know why it is only our privilege to risk our lives for people we don't even know? Why doesn't he choose others instead of us for this journey?"

He focused his attention on the sky, as if trying to find the answer to all these questions.

After a few minutes, I replied: "The wisdom of God is greater than that of men, Dimi. It is better to answer 'yes' and say 'amen' to what he wants us to do. I'm not the best person to enlighten you about all these questions; that's why we have so many men of God who have accompanied us throughout this fight. We should simply give thanks to him and submit to his will."

I told the Apostle Isaac first, without even wanting to know the identity of the other people chosen to accompany Dimi on this voyage. After this news, we spent three days fasting because we knew that the separation wouldn't be too easy. We wanted above all to receive divine protection that would diminish any doubts in our minds. Because of this sudden departure, we didn't want to be mistaken about the individuals who would take part in the crossing. Eight men and four women were chosen to go. Our return was another mystery as we were facing some overly direct questions from our loved ones. We couldn't answer any of them. Dimitrova was, of course, the first one chosen. Much to my amazement, the Apostle Isaac was chosen as was my elder brother Jimmy, Pastor Hinn, Pastor Osteen and Pastor Lucado. Leonardo DiCaprio, one of Jack's best friends and also the godfather of one of my twins, was also part of the group. The former President Obama, who had come out of nowhere, the former French President Sarkozy, who followed my advice from the very beginning, all had settled in Percé with us. Of the Jewish religion, the latter had always respected my Christian faith. For a quite a long time, I had known that he was working on behalf of many good causes, but I could never have imagined that he would also be taken. This was the last name for the men's section. I always had huge doubts about God's choices of whom he would send to fulfill this prophecy, but I had still not understood the fact that he does not choose like a mere mortal would. I had been watching all of us since the beginning of the war and often wondered in silence which of these men and women would be willing to leave without any constraints, leaving behind families and children. I had always ruled out the possibility that my sisters and I were perhaps the key to the doors of Etener's mystery. I think that deep down, I had already known since I was seven years old the answer to some of these questions. I had made tremendous sacrifices for a time because it was necessary to reunite each of my younger sisters and prepare them for this specific purpose. I knew that what we had experienced after so many years had been a kind of test that prepared us for this voyage. It was the Legend of the sisters' souls, the work I had created early in my career, except that it was a little different from the book and was now happening with the Third World War. God wanted us to experience it. For what purpose? Unfortunately, I did not have all the answers. But I was exercising some patience toward the end, more than anyone else, to finally discover what I am now called to make you understand. I understood the pain in the eyes of those who would feel abandoned as soon as we had left. My heart broke into a thousand pieces to abandon my twins and my husband, who were not taking part in the journey. He did not understand this madness and said that I was simply a neglectful mother who was ready to abandon my family for what many considered a lost cause. I kept crying and praying that my husband forgive me, hoping that he would replace me as best he could with my girls. I had never seen my mother panic so much as at the thought of suddenly losing all her daughters at the same time. Because once she knew what was really happening, she implored us to change our minds, forgetting all our good principles for the cause. My children and sisters had become increasingly inconsolable when they understood the extent of the problem. Each of us had to overcome anguish from our loved ones. But once the decision was made, we all knew that it was irrefutable. Coinciden-tally, one of the boats left the dock to go back out to sea; when we told them that we were seeking to embark with them, it was as if they already knew about it. They in no way prevented us from taking part in the journey.

In two days, on November 11th, 2029, twelve of us would be aboard the W. US NAVY ship, and our destination would be the unknown, with the hope of finding a second world. I could not sleep the two nights before we left. I wanted to enjoy every moment surrounded by my loved ones without being able to let go of them for a second. We spent the last day together, grouped together hand in hand in a circle, and we prayed for hours, joined together with one heart. For the first time, Mr. Obama and his two daughters, his lovely wife and his five grandchildren had joined us. He had aged and still seemed worried most of the time. Who could have blamed him? His two sons-in-law had been chosen from the start to lead troops in Asia. His daughters were always courageous, but their eyes betrayed their state of mind. I was well placed to understand because of the letter sent to Jack two years earlier, when I knew he was leaving for the war. I was inconsolable for more than a month, but when he underwent medical tests before his departure—thank God!—his heart seemed too fragile for such troubles. They sent him home. He took it very personally because it was a blow to his ego. Later, he saw how lucky he was to not have taken part in that disaster. Jack had always been a reasonable man, which is why he had ended up accepting the decision, seeing that he wasn't the only one affected by this departure, and I felt more grateful to God for the way he worked in each case. At the dawn of our much-anticipated departure, we boarded the W. US NAVY, leaving the dock sooner than we had hoped. I felt an infinite sadness, and I didn't know what to think of it all.

I was looking into the distance when Pastor Hinn approached me and spoke to me in these terms:

"You're a very strange woman."

I turned to gaze at him with tear-filled eyes.

—"Why make such a remark?" I asked the dying old man, who had accepted for better or worse to take part in this strange voyage with us.

—"You could have simply refused everything and dissuaded your sisters at the same time. You are young, and we would have understood, but despite it all, you showed immense courage, and you came with them. You alone, you undergirded the resoluteness of their decision and, together, you had the courage to leave behind your unhappy children and husbands."

He touched my shoulder while shaking his head as if he saw something more than a simple little woman with sadness in her eyes. I had all the trouble in the world convincing Deborah, who had become inconsolable about leaving her newborn; tirelessly, I had begged her to understand the mission and the cause I was fighting for. Once the other parts of the world were destroyed, I knew that it would be a matter of time before it would be

Percé's turn to disappear. We would have perished with the others because we would not have had the courage to get out of our miserable little life to fight the good fight. Lindsay had been logical as usual, and Jenny was the only one to be a little more enthusiastic than the others because her husband was also part of the journey. The beginning of a big change would begin with this voyage, and six years were about to make us into one family united by a single God. I was overjoyed that my brother was part of this small group; I somehow felt safer. I think I had requested this in my prayers, and I was more than grateful for this favour. Pastor Hinn was the oldest and wisest of us, but at times when I observed him, I was worried about him more than anyone, wondering how he would be able to keep up with us. I knew that if God had chosen him, it was because he would be able to complete this journey. I only prayed that we would all arrive safe and sound at our destination, and I couldn't question such an important decision. Each of us had been chosen for a specific purpose, and I felt it from the depths of my heart.

We ate very little, prayed a lot and were lacking sleep most of the time. After two long months, we arrived at our destination, the port of Pennsylvania, in the United States of America. With my sisters, I was finally able to renew our old bonds during the first week we spent on the boat. We laughed our way through our troubles, and being connected to each other, we were especially ready to face Lucifer himself. I was just calculating in my mind, sixty-one of the three thousand one hundred eighty days had passed. Three thousand one hundred nineteen days of this very, very long expedition remained. We had celebrated Christmas and New Year's on that cursed ship while sparing ourselves the thought that a missile could have

destroyed us at any time. It was the first Christmas without my family, but it would not be my last one, I encouraged myself with each passing day. I had a little notebook where I reported everything that was happening at the end of each day. I was beginning to terribly miss my little girls, and nothing I could do would fill the huge void in my heart and mind. If we were six years away from reaching our destination, I was really starting to wonder what would happen from now until then. Why couldn't we take a plane and cut this long trip in half? I wasn't too sure that I understood the magnitude of our mission.

When we landed at the dock of Pennsylvania, a few large officers in charge of security let us pass without any trouble. They were surprised to see us together without a bodyguard, but since we had long ago become public figures with a mission of another significance, we had no problem. To our amazement, they asked for our prayers, and we acceded to their requests right away. Many soldiers appeared to be already dying. They looked at us, my sisters and me, with eyes full of questions about how long the war would last. We spent the night with them, and the next day, we found a small plane that was leaving in the direction of Cape Verde. We knew that a good opportunity was presenting itself to us because they had come to offer it to us as if they had been waiting for us for a long time. We flew over the North Atlantic Ocean, and we had a stopover in Morocco, which was in midst of the war. I had not understood why we were going through Morocco until we came upon someone who had become a great servant of God many years ago, Rachid Badouri. He had moved with his small family six years before the declaration of war, and he had never been able to leave after it broke out. This was not a coincidence since he knew we would come. The day before, we had appeared before him in a dream, just when he had asked God for help before going to bed. It was the second bomb that Morocco had endured in less than six months and a third would end up completely destroying it. No planes were landing there. We hurried to bring him, his wife and fourteen-year-old daughter on board with us, over the objections of the pilot who was threatening to leave us on the ground. We quickly left after filling the small plane with the needed fuel. Once we arrived in Cape Verde, he left us there, and we continued the journey on our own. We had increased in number, and this did not make the trip easier, but it wasn't our cause—it was God's. We simply followed his plans. The Apostle was overjoyed at the reunion with his spiritual son whom he had not seen since a long time before the war. He had undoubtedly missed him, and their mutual joy was a pleasure to witness. The father finally found his long-lost son.

We couldn't leave Cape Verde because of the town's destruction. We were pained to see the number of deaths caused by one of the missiles sent by Russia, according to survivors in the region. They were mourning their lost families. When I looked at them more closely, I felt they were expecting the rest of the city's annihilation. I couldn't be there without doing anything. I comforted the children who had become neglected orphans as best I could by attending to their various injuries. The girls and I had long taken first-aid training, and together, we provided what little help we could by bringing comfort to as many people as possible. We were starting to pray together when a miracle occurred at the moment when it was least expected. Since the bomb had destroyed everything in its path, there were no more water sources, and the earth began to dry up. At a specific moment, Pastor Hinn touched the ground and water flowed forth. The inhabitants, who were astonished, came to us and expected us to bring back the dead. Unfortunately, it was

impossible since they were already dead, and we were not God. One after another, they drank the water and thanked us many times for our kindness. We were anxious to know when we could leave this place. We couldn't do anything but wait, hoping to quickly find a solution. Despite everything, we stayed there for seven days. The last day, to our great joy, a large Canadian Armed Forces aircraft came to bring aid and food for victims in the area. The crew was surprised to find us in such a place. They had to leave in the evening and asked us to come on board with them; they would stop in Mali for two weeks and land in Egypt to close out their adventure. It was perfect for us since we were heading in the same destination.

The flight in question lasted two days and as we landed in Mali, we noticed that the condition of the inhabitants was no better than those in Cape Verde. They looked at us as if we were from another planet, which was to be expected, given their condition. I again pitied those people, and I couldn't imagine anything worse than their living conditions. The city was cut in two, and no one could jump across the huge crevasse separating the two parts of the city. This new situation prevented families who were still alive from coming together. They looked at each other from afar without being able to do anything to change the harsh reality of the situation. They were all afraid of falling into the void if they decided to jump over this hole, which measured at least eight hundred kilometres in length. I asked the pilot why he wasn't doing anything to reunite these families, and he responded:

"Count yourself lucky, my dear lady,that I have taken you up to here." "You believe in God," he added sarcastically, "so it's up to you to make such a miracle happen. We just follow orders and reuniting families is not our mission."

I couldn't believe that I was hearing him speak this way, but I knew that I shouldn't make a scene, which would slow us down. I shared this with the Apostle who, in turn, was treated in the same way as I had been. After a week of prayers, we were able to make the officials in charge of the flight change their minds and help people who still had family cross over to the other side. The only satisfaction that we had from this long journey was the little good that we were doing when we could. I felt great joy in watching the others, who were smiling through their sorrow. Communications had been cut off for security reasons in some states, and none of us could reach our family members. Our living conditions were a miracle every day compared to the rest of the survivors, who were dying of hunger, lack of medical care and even grief. I realized how lucky I was to be in good health. I was one of those chosen from an entire nation to fulfill the destiny of the whole world.

Among the Malians, there was a little girl that I felt was different from the others. I didn't speak of it to anyone, and I continued to observe her from a distance for three days. She was always alone, which indicated to me that she had become an orphan. She also followed us but never had the nerve to approach and risk being rejected. I felt I had no right to leave her to that terrible fate. I had not noticed, while I was watching the girl, that Lindsay, who knew me better than anyone, felt my concern for this child. On the fourth day, she approached me and whispered, "What you're feeling inside, we also feel it."

She pointed at Jenny and Deb, who turned around at the same time, as if connected to each difficult event that I was going through without understanding. She turned, gazed again at the little girl in the distance and continued, "I think she is one of those people for whom we are making this long journey, if you want my opinion."

I turned, surprised to find that I wasn't the only one thinking it, and I replied:

"She has a magnetism that I can't ignore, and I have been wondering for three days

whether I should talk to someone else about what I'm feeling.

—There is nothing to say. We're not fools. I'm sure you can make the right choice.

With that, I left my sister, and I decided to go find the little girl because time was passing, and we would soon be leaving for Egypt. When I was close to her, she kept her calm. I understood that she also had been waiting impatiently for that moment.

"Hello," I said, kindly. I didn't know if she was able to understand me, but to my amazement, she said in perfect English, "Hello."

She dared not look me in the eye, and I felt more love for her shyness mixed with remarkable wisdom.

"You don't have to lower your eyes, I won't hurt you."

—"I know, I'm not scared of you because I know who you are."

—"Oh yeah?" I said, taken aback by her response. "And now, tell me who am I supposed to be?"

—"My parents called you 'the converted saint.'"

I had never heard someone use such a name to describe me, and I imagined that she and her family had probably read my books.

"You know, we can just talk to each other as friends. Now, tell me, how old are you?"

—"I just turned twelve a month ago."

—"Where are your parents?"

—"They died while trying to rescue my little sister," she sorrowfully confided to me."

On many occasions, I could have died like her parents and left my little girls behind. Thinking about what she must have been through, my heart sank even further.

"What, is your name, my dear?

—"Élisabeth," she replied with dignity.

—"Élisabeth, how did you know I would come?" I became curious about this part, which I just couldn't understand.

—"I saw you appear on a white horse two years ago. I told my parents, who didn't want to believe me. I eventually forgot my dream and thought they were right. I wanted to die with them when they were gone. They didn't even say goodbye. I had decided to drink a few lethal drinks that my dad had in his lab, but I fainted before doing it. While I was still conscious, I had that same dream. Then you appeared on the plane over there," she said, pointing to the white aircraft.

The white horse, I thought.

"If I asked you to come with me, Élisabeth, could I count on you to be a part of our team in this adventure?"

—"Yes!" she exclaimed joyfully without the trace of a doubt. "Anyway, I have no one else in the world," she said sadly.

—"Do you believe in God, Élisabeth?"

—"Yes, and I always knew he was protecting me. When I was born, I couldn't walk, and all the doctors said that I would stay like that, but one day an angel came, and he cured me by touching my legs. The next day, I rose from my bed talking about what I'd seen, and I could walk, run, jump and dance."

She smiled thinking back to the old memories that she carefully safeguarded in her memory. That little girl ended up conquering my heart and what I now had to do was announce to the others the arrival of my new protégé, whom I felt was another chosen one in God's plan. I lost no time in gathering the entire group to tell them about what I had just experienced while introducing Élisabeth, who was shier than ever. Listening to the story of that little girl, they could only agree with my final decision. I spent almost all my time talking with the little one. I introduced her to my sisters, who immediately fell under her spell. Three days after we met, she made her official entry by following us into the plane sent by the Canadian Government that was leaving for Egypt. She didn't let go of my hand for a second as she clutched it in hers for the entire trip. I knew that this little girl had strangely become another member of my family. I already couldn't wait to introduce her to my husband.

Eight hours later, we landed at a small airport built for the war; this short, ordinary flight would have lasted five hours under normal circumstances. The pilot explained that because of air patrols, everything had become very complicated for the last two months. Once there, the situation seemed much better than anything that we had experienced since the beginning of our journey. Given the circumstances and being in enemy territory, my sisters and I were dressed like all the other women in the country. Which is why our hair and faces could under no circumstances be seen. We asked for transport, but unfortunately, cars had become a luxury. The roads were too dangerous because of the bombs and traps that were set everywhere. Dimitrova suggested that we continue alone along the coast of Egypt to the Nile Basin. I knew that the Nile ran through Rwanda, Burundi, Tanzania, Uganda, Ethiopia, South Sudan and also Egypt. The Nile was the means of transportation of the Egyptians in the past. The mystery that remained to be known was exactly where we were going. We knew that this might be very dangerous, but since we held him in such high respect and had so much trust in him, we all ended up agreeing with his decision. We walked to the point of exhaustion, crossing the Sahara Desert for over ten days. In the beginning, with money that we had brought for special situations, since we had no other choice, we paid for huge camels that completed just half the journey with us. They stopped, exhausted by the lack of food and water, and we had to leave them behind and continue on the rest of the way on our own.

If I were to start talking about each of those endless days, I would never finish talking about those six years of travel! There were, however, the three long days when I fell ill and thought I would no longer see the end of the journey. Eyes closed, I relived some parts of my life that I was no longer proud of because I quite often wondered if things would have been different if I had acted differently. I prayed constantly about the things that were not so kosher that I had done in my and others' lives, such as the way that I had steered my sisters' lives. Until Dimitrova, I was always in my sister Jenny's way, undermining all those endeavours that I almost never approved of. Deborah, the most rebellious one, always gave me trouble. I had ended up forcing them all to sign contracts that let me take care of managing their lives. In the eyes of the media, I had become the mini Kris Jenner in the life of my little sisters, and I squeezed all the money I could out of this situation. This did not last very long, but I really acquired a taste for it. I ended up divorcing Sylvano during the second year of our life together, and I went to live in the United States with my sisters, despite all his pleas. I had little use for expecting anything from a man whom I felt was eager to deceive me whenever I turned my back. His past criminal record had not helped our cause since he couldn't go with me on tour in the States. Our arguments made me sick, and I needed, as my mother had advised me, to get away. I could have stayed and saved my marriage, but I opted for the easiest decision because I knew that it would have been his life versus mine. I broke his heart, and I had been sorry to see his life turn into a nightmare after my departure. I had obsessively loved him, and today it meant nothing because he was no longer with me. I had never stopped thinking about him, or even praying for him so that he would be spared and be safe wherever he was. I had not always been a saint, you know, and I didn't realize it until that moment of agony.

Despite always silent being so silent, Badouri's wife Julie was an angel because most of the time it was she who stayed with me. On the fourth day, when I started to feel much better, I promised myself to change my ways once and for all when all this would end. Maybe someday I will specifically write a book just about the days that we spent along the road to the Nile Basin. For the time being, I just need to tell you that we found very little food, and we were starting to think that we were perhaps at the end of our lives when we finally saw the beginning of the basin in the distance. It was DiCaprio's turn to fall ill two days after I had recovered. We were seriously worried about how to transport him despite his many objections. His condition was growing worse, but when I saw the Nile, I thought it would be a chance to heal him. I knew an old Egyptian myth about the Nile Basin that spoke of healing, but I knew it was just a myth. I couldn't show my tremendous fear to the others, and especially not to the children who looked to us as an example. I had the impression that we must all dive into the Nile, and above all Leo, who was in the most need. I told them my idea and a little story about the healing powers of the Egyptian basin. Jenny, who didn't speak much, thought that my idea was profound, and Pastor Lucado confirmed that it pleased him. Once in front of this vast basin, which covers more than three million two hundred thousand square kilometres, we were afraid of drowning. Leo, who absolutely wanted to return to his previous state, asked to be immersed in it. Without waiting a minute longer, my brother stepped forward to go down into it with him so that nothing would befall him. Once they had come back out, we found that each was feeling better than he had before. I saw them feeling so good that I too thought about drinking that water. Instinctively, I knew that this gesture would boost my knowledge about all that escaped me about life in general. My sisters followed my example and encouraged the others to do the same. Logically, we knew we were supernaturally protected. We were grateful to see the magic of this blessing at the end of each day. We couldn't move forward or travel six thousand seven hundred kilometres to get to the other side of the River, so we decided to camp not far from there with the hope that another miracle would soon occur.

This river was helping us understand the most ancient mysteries of previous ages and centuries about the Pharaoh himself; as the magic of the water worked its way through our organs and expanded our vision, we felt greatly energized. Finally, half of us had opted for a nap. I couldn't follow suit. I was too concerned about what would happen if we perished by the Nile. I continued to thank the Lord, but at the same time, I asked him to bless us so that we would quickly find some help. We were all hungry, and resting in a warmer, more comfortable place would have been greatly appreciated. Distractedly, I looked out into the distance, and I saw a little canoe that could carry at least six people coming. I told myself that my imagination was probably playing tricks on me without, however, looking away. With relief, I suddenly rose when I saw it coming toward where we were. The canoe seemed so small that I wondered how we could all cross the river at the same time. However, I was hoping that the boatman would be able to help us. We no longer had any gold or silver, and I was worried what he would ask for in return for transporting us. Quietly, the small vessel approached the shore. I didn't expect to see a dwarf who was half my size, let alone see him pointing a gun at us! Even though he wore a disguise, I realized that I had already seen him somewhere. When the memory came back to me, I remembered exactly where it came from. What I didn't know, however, was why it was necessary to come across him. I wasn't one of his close friends, but I knew him very well. Leonardo and my husband talked to him from time to time when he was in town.

I thought that he had surely been kidnapped, but to see his military camouflage, I determined that he too was trying to find his way. He was an American in Egyptian lands on a small boat travelling the Nile Basin. Decidedly, I hadn't yet seen it all! Deborah, who had risen immediately after me and who was watching what was happening, shouted his name as if to convince herself that it was not some sick joke of nature. He answered, "yes," motioning not to talk too loudly; he seemed even more shaken by his own experiences. It was Peter Dinklage in person. For all of you who are asking questions, let me take this chance to introduce you to the formerly famous character who became the most famous man in the story since his appearance on Game of Thrones. When he saw us, and he recognized us without our veils, his reaction was the same as mine, and while I wasn't expecting this gesture, he jumped into my arms and did the same to Leo and my brother when he saw them. I could see his joy, and I was, to be honest, thrilled to come upon him in such circumstances. We were all shaken by such a stunning turn of events. Without giving us time to say anything, he started up the conversation.

"I wasn't sure that I understood my mission up to this point, but now that I see you, I think that everything is becoming clearer.

"How do you explain your premonitions, Peter?" I asked him, surprised at what I heard coming from his mouth.

"I came here with American troops two days ago. We were violently attacked, and I escaped by finding this small boat not far from where I was hiding. I lost consciousness once on board when a bullet hit me in the back. I felt it rip through my back, and I fainted, but I think that my time had not yet come. Believe it or not, an angel appeared to me. I thought that I was dead, and I was so scared. He touched my back and finally said that he was only there to protect me. In turn, I was to travel along the shore and rescue people who had a crucial mission, he told me. A mission in which I was chosen to become one of the guardians of the mystery." He paused to ask, before continuing his story: "Would someone kindly tell me exactly what kind of mystery it is? I must be extremely lucky not to be dead right now. I had regained consciousness for only a few minutes; when I saw you, I was still afraid that you are part of the enemy camp. I can assure you that I was never so happy to see people I know in my entire life."

His last comment made us all laugh. We were happy to have come across him, and we explained to him what we were doing in the middle of nowhere, without neglecting to mention the purpose of our mission. I understand the trouble he had in processing what he had heard. I told him that nothing forced him to take part in this journey unless he really wanted to. For some people, it amounted to complete suicide, but the fact is that we were all still alive, and we absolutely wanted to continue to the end. I saw him watch the other members of the group, and he seemed to ask a lot of questions. He knew who we were and had gone through a very unsettling experience, but he worked up his courage toward the end, and agreed to come after a few minutes of reflection. He wanted to join our little group, which didn't stop growing.

I knew that we still had to cross, and I knew that it would be no easy matter because of our numbers. We would not all succeed in boarding the small boat, and this was a huge problem. We asked him various questions about what there was on the other side of the Nile where he had come from. He told us about the trick that the Russians had used to eliminate the American base. We would not be safe if we crossed over onto that shore of the river, he eventually divulged in complete sincerity.

We knew that following the Nile we could go to Al Qahirah, also known as Cairo, but we were not sure about what would await us in the capital of a country full of wrongdoers. We had to do this trip twice, leaving half of us, and then transporting the other half of our crew. We really had no choice, and we sent six of us as well as Peter, who wasn't heavy, in the first crossing. We were hoping he would agree to make the trip again to pick up the others. Deb, Elizabeth, my brother, Leo, Pastor Hinn, the Apostle Isaac and I remained behind for the second crossing. I let my other two sisters go with great difficulty, praying that everything would go well for each member of the group. We spent the day waiting for the return of the small boat that didn't reappear until the next day at dawn. I could only thank Peter, who had again volunteered to transport us, embracing him with even more enthusiasm. We wanted to know how he was taking this abrupt change of scenario in his life. He didn't know how to answer the question. He eventually admitted to us,

"I have committed so many sins in my life that, for me, this is a way to redeem myself, to make sure that I have a small place among the best of all those who are destined to receive mercy in the eyes of he whose patience has reached its limit. He's now watching us kill each other, and I imagine that he has no use in interfering in our lives because we are doing what we thought was best for us and for others. He has again given me a second chance, so I am proving to him that he wasn't mistaken in doing so."

He had somehow seen clearly, and I could only thank him of his realization. He could have simply decided not to get involved in this cause that was not entirely his own. We wasted no time getting on board. We suggested that he rest shortly after he had informed us about the way to go. The voyage in such a small, narrow space was so long and uncomfortable that the mission to reach the others was almost impossible. I had a premonition that something serious was about to happen. I dared not to share it with the others for fear of worrying them over nothing, but Deb felt it as much as I did and said so as she whispered in my ear. The Nile had become more dangerous because water had grown choppy, but we continued to move forward, hoping to arrive as quickly as possible. I shook Peter, who, for a few minutes, had fallen more deeply asleep than we had expected. When he opened his eyes, he wanted to know for how long we had let him rest, with a confusion that spoke volumes about the extent of the problem. "20 minutes or so," I replied, concerned about the expression on his face; my premonition no longer surprised me! He then checked before confirming that we were not going in the right direction. My brother, stunned and tired of playing the hero, started to let himself get carried away in anger. We tried to reason with him by explaining in vain that it wasn't really the fault of anyone in particular. We could have just turned back, but the problem was that we didn't know where to direct the small boat. We eventually decided to maneuver the boat but without great success. At that moment, we lost control because of the strength of the current, which was pushing us harder and harder toward a gigantic waterfall, much to our dismay. We screamed in terror like hunted animals, which changed absolutely nothing—the boat was smashed, and we plunged into the unknown.

I remember waking up a few hours later with a painful body, shouting the few names that I could still remember. I continued screaming as loud as I could without getting an answer. I couldn't believe that our trip was taking such a catastrophic turn. I had to at least find the survivors. I was crying, thinking that we could not have had as much bad luck as this situation, when, suddenly, Peter grabbed my arm, gesturing that I should be quiet. We were not alone, we had never been and that was the reason why the others had not replied. I realized too late, because in a very short, time soldiers surrounded us from all sides. I had alerted them by my screams while I was looking for everyone else. They had lit up intense lights that they were shining in our direction. My heart was beating so fast that I was expecting it to stop at any moment. At that moment, I wanted to no longer exist—I started with my prayers deep inside and I was no longer able to stop. I was imagining what these people would eventually put us through when they captured us. I was thinking about a million things at once when I saw a big machine gun right in front of my eyes and, without expecting it, I lost consciousness. I had never fainted until that day, but I knew that it would end up happening one day or another. I was one of those women who can't think anymore when I panicked. We had landed in the enemy's jaws, and I couldn't understand the reason for this reversal of fortune. They managed to find all of us, which was not a good thing because I imagined that our first group would no longer be able to continue their journey without wanting to come get us. I had hoped that they would return with help, but I could only leave that to God himself. Of course, when they captured us, some soldiers recognized those who had become celebrities many years ago. They would not have let us go under any circumstances for the simple reason that Mr. Obama, Leo, Peter and Pastor Hinn were Americans. We all represented too large a sum of money in their eyes. Personally, I was still in shock. I didn't admit it, but I felt safer being with my friends. We spent the night not exactly tied up from head to foot, but let's just say that we were not really able to go anywhere. I didn't know where we were or where they were taking us. They boarded us into a big truck and brought us back with them. I did not understand the dialect that these soldiers were using among themselves, but I understood, however, the joy they were taking in looking at the women. Their eyes said a lot about what they would do if no one was giving them orders. My blood gradually froze as I went to their quarters. I was wondering how we could get out of this place alive. I was in Egypt with friends who were war prisoners like me. Tears ran silently from my eyes as I thought about the family that I might never again see. Once at the base, about 30 minutes from the scene of the accident, they locked us in a small cell pending the arrival of one of their commanders, who would decide what would happen to all of us.

Before I continue, I must digress about an important part of this story. When I was just a mere cabaret dancer, I met a man in one of the ritziest clubs on Stanley Street in downtown Montreal. One night, I saw him enter the club. He was one of those men who did not go unnoticed. Basically, he was a very handsome man. From the moment he saw me, he felt a very strong attraction that I wasn't indifferent to either. He motioned for me to come see him and did not take long in telling me about some very interesting aspects of his life. He was an important man who ran one of the most renowned banks in Egypt. He wanted to pay so that his pleasure with me would last until the next morning. He paid for my entire evening just so that I would keep him company. At the end of the evening, he still offered me yet another sum of money that I didn't want to refuse. He wanted me to spend the night in his company without obligating me to fall in love. All night, he took a lot of cocaine without trying to touch me. At the time, I thought that this man didn't come from the same planet, and I even remember that, the next day, I asked him if he planned to come and settle down in Montreal one of these days. In fact, he kept his word, and paid me everything he owed me the next day. I had fallen asleep at his side waiting for the sunrise without a worry about being in danger with him. I went my separate way from him, and I never had heard anything about him until that day.

We were in prison waiting to be accused of who knows what when I saw the Egyptian officer in question approach my cell. I had never been able to forget his face, and I think the same could be said for him. I watched him confusedly glancing back and forth between Deb and me because of our great resemblance. Thank God, he had become the commander in chief of the Egyptian army. He still looked like the jovial man whom I had met a few years before. I had not really aged and still looked like the one who had charmed him in the very beginning. He stepped closer, and I saw that the memory was coming back to him, except that he couldn't tell which of us was the right one. He couldn't show any emotion for the prisoners they captured. Noticing his confusion at what he was seeing, I approached him timidly with a sudden confidence in life. Without hesitating, he asked me to meet in his office to question me personally. He cast a quick glance at each person in the cell without speaking a word, and he turned around as if he had just come across a ghost. No one could know what had really happened between me and this man a few years previously. No soldier could challenge his request by refusing to let me see him, so they asked me to follow them without any other explanation. We had the same reaction of surprise, and I was now wondering what would happen once I was with him. He could have changed for the worse, or the other way around, which would not have surprised me, but the main thing was that I had happened upon the chance of my lifetime. I entered his tent, and he asked the officer behind me to leave us alone. "Hello, Madame Châtel," he said in perfect French with a simple smile. "To what do we owe this honour in such circumstances?" I returned his smile despite all the pain in my muscles, and I replied, "A mission from God, quite simply."

—"Oh yes, that's it! But why Egypt?"

—"Because we really had no choice since all routes were destroyed because of this war." I didn't want to talk about things that we already both knew. How are you?" He looked at me as if we had just run into each other yesterday and replied in the same friendly tone, "I'm not well at all. I command a bunch of losers who have no choice, just like me." I was genuinely sorry to see him show me his real face filled with fear and shame. I quietly approached him. I wanted to show him that I could still give him a big hug without us killing each other as others have been doing in recent years. He gladly accepted my drawing close to him and very politely took me in his arms. I saw that he was on the edge of the abyss, and I felt sorry for him. He stepped aside as if to warn me that we had to be careful to not be caught in this position. I understood him only too well. He regained his seriousness, "Tell me, what are you doing in this kind of place, Leonardo DiCaprio, that dying old man and the other prisoners who are with you? And the one who is a mirror image of you? I thought that I was hallucinating," he eventually added, seeming worried.

Without wasting any time, I again explained what we were doing there and the purpose of our trip. I mentioned the presence of the others that we had lost along the way. All this seemed like an unreal story, but who would not have been able to believe that there may be another chance for people, like him or me, to escape such an ending?

"I can help you get out of here, but I can't guarantee to help those who have gotten lost, Mel. Plus, Sarkozy and Obama are statesmen that everyone is looking for right now. But why, for goodness' sake, are you going on such a dangerous journey?"

"Come with us," I proposed to him without directly answering his question.

"Even if I wanted to, I'd automatically become a deserter, and anyone could shoot me. They are not the ones who will decide your fate, but He, up above, is. I'd like to believe in Him, but things have become too complicated down here. You're wondering why, among all the other officers, I came across you and not someone else? I prefer not to understand the reason, but I can tell you that if it's because of Him. He is too strong. I'll have to send you back to your cell because, given the hour, they must all be asking themselves questions about the time we have taken to talk."

"OK," I answered simply, understanding what he was referring to.

"All the same, could you do something for those we have lost?"

"I'll see, but for now, I can't do anything."

—"Thank you. "May God bless you and protect you so that you do not lose your soul, my dear friend," I said with a look of compassion that expressed my gratitude.

He called the nearby soldier on duty and asked him to take me back to my cell. I thanked God for each of his opportunities, thinking that the worst had been avoided. I told my friends of my meeting with the Commander with the utmost discretion. In turn, they could scarcely believe our luck. Their concerns were the same as mine with regards to the assistance he could provide to the others. We weren't too sure what would happen if they too were caught. All that we hoped was that they would not be as unlucky as we were. We didn't wait for our liberation for long. The Commander had kept his word once again and even insisted on accompanying us to find the others. He had the use of one of his big tanks, and we travelled a long way along the Nile in an hour and a half. Unfortunately, we didn't find them anywhere. We were turning back when we saw another truck with the same troops as ours transporting other prisoners who closely resembled the ones in our group. I quickly rose, asking them to stop without even worrying about what could have happened to me. The Commander followed me and in turn, with his hands, motioned for them to stop the truck. He checked with me and, touching his arm, I confirmed that I wasn't mistaken. He ordered them to release the prisoners by explaining the situation in their own language. He avoided providing too many details because he did not want us to be suspected of treason or something similar. The others had lived through an entirely different experience than we had. Recognizing us, they eagerly leaped to embrace us and began saying some hallelujahs in all directions. I couldn't have been more grateful to this man that God had allowed me to find after so many years. Sarkozy and Obama were barely recognizable, which was a very good thing. The small group joined ours and without waiting a minute longer, we made our way to Cairo, the capital and largest city in Egypt. We were forced to go back again because the commander had informed us that a small plane would leave the same day for Israel. Once in Cairo, he waited with us for an hour while getting to know my other sisters, who charmed him. We were sad to see the very small aircraft land on the airstrip that was going to take us toward the next destination that we had never visited before. I thought, as I stood up before boarding, that we couldn't be more blessed than we had been. I was not overlooking the fact that we had repeatedly survived near-death experiences. I spoke with the commander for almost the whole time to try to convince him to go with us or even to meet us in Israel. He looked at me and repeated with a smile, "I have to make sure I'm still here if ever you get captured again. That way, I will have the same power to free you yet another time." I observed his face, which had become serious again, as if he wanted to leave everything and go on our adventure. I felt sorry for him without saying so to him. I couldn't imagine a worse prison than his. He was in a war that was not his cause, and he was making himself lead because millions of lives were under his command. He felt obliged to take them to the front because he considered himself above all a patriot. He squeezed my hand and asked me to be careful and look after the others. I kissed him on both cheeks, promising that he would be in my prayers from now on. Very sad because of the latest events that I had just experienced, I followed the others inside the aircraft. I looked at everyone without saying anything and walked to the back because I wanted a reflective moment to myself. I knew that other things might happen, and I was unconsciously preparing to face all eventualities. I saw that the others were showing me even more respect, and I didn't take any pride in it, thinking that everything was happening for a specific reason. How I could have known that man didn't matter to me anymore because, ultimately, I realized that our meeting had been planned from the beginning. It took three hours to arrive in Israel with a lot of bumps that made me sick with the thought that our small plane would end up crashing before landing. We landed as fast as possible while thanking the pilot for his generosity before wishing him good luck. He had to return to Cairo because he had been called again for a new flight. He did not really leave us any choice but to cut short any conversation that would put him in danger because he was wiretapped at all times. By making signs whenever we engaged in any conversation, we eventually understood what he was trying to show us. We were left in the middle of nature, and we put our lives in the hands of He who had asked us to undertake the long journey. We spoke neither Hebrew nor Arabic, but we found a young boy who was fluent in French. We proposed to him that he come to Jerusalem with us. We were in a dangerous place, bombarded by enemy countries. We did not discuss his warnings, knowing that he was best placed to get us through this remote part of Israel that we were unfamiliar with. It was the second time that I had come to Israel, and I think I far preferred the first; I wasn't feeling so much confidence this time. Almost everything had been destroyed, and the town itself looked like a mobile ruin. I did not understand why the world had become so cruel. It was obvious that the demon had begun his work. He was growing in depth and breadth as far as the eye could see. Jerusalem was not so far from where we had been led. Twenty minutes were enough for us to make our appearance by walking cautiously. We were stopped more than once, but before leaving Cairo, the Commander had given me an official letter attesting that we represented no threat. He advised me to use it when I felt any danger approaching. Whenever I showed the letter, they didn't try to retain us and let us leave immediately with much more kindness, as if they felt that we represented hope for the suffering people. We were led into neighborhoods that had recently been named the Surfts of Jerusalem. They consisted of a few buildings stuffed full with those who had been wounded in the war. They wanted to take advantage of our presence and begged us to help those who were suffering so terribly. They explained to us that they did not have enough nurses on their teams because of the staff who were perishing from all kinds of attacks. I wondered if staying and helping these people was also part of this mission. The answer was obvious since we had become envoys of light who must save lives. Jenny was the first to respond quickly before all the others. Her decision left us no choice but to submit to this sudden wish to help. We put on the scrubs for this task, and even though we didn't know where to start. After a few minutes, we found something to do. We realized that we could not have abandoned so many people to such a sad fate. The more involved we became, the more days went by without us being able to leave Jerusalem. Most of us were known as foreign aid workers, and we were delighted to provide some well-being to those people. We had been winning the respect and love of all since our arrival. No other flight was able to take us anywhere. It was as if it was necessary for us to stay longer.

The rules could not be questioned. All those who were not married could not sleep together and for the others, a small room was granted them. The women slept with women and men with men. I had not left Élisabeth's side for a single moment. I didn't trust anyone. And especially not those men who would have sold their souls to have a small piece of fresh meat to satisfy their animal instincts. We were at war, and we could not think for one second that this could change anything for some people. Only Jenny and Dimi benefited from the tiny privilege of coming together in the evening to sleep. As for my two sisters, even if they did not often complain, they did not like to sleep so close together. They did not hesitate to voice their discontent; they resented me for convincing them to embark on this suicidal adventure. Mr. Obama, as I have always called him, was still in a good mood. He had been getting along very well with Sarkozy since the start of the trip. The two were inseparable, as were Élisabeth and Rachid's daughter. Absolutely nothing surprised me when I saw bonds like these form between us. Personally, I loved talking with the Pastor Hinn, Leo and Peter when the opportunity arose. The same small plane that had transported us from Cairo returned, but my request that we be taken somewhere else and away from Jerusalem remained unanswered. No one could leave for at least six months, and I was all worked up about having to continue eating poorly and sleeping in such a primitive way. I was aware of how lucky I was to be free and to act as I wished without being locked up in a cell. I just had to accept events as they came and bide my time. At first, we completely changed the way we prayed. Toward the end of the first month, we respectfully agreed to accept all the Jews who wanted to join and participate in our hymns and worship. We concluded that staying too long in such a place could not be a mere coincidence. We began to preach the Gospel despite many threats and protests by disgruntled fanatics. I was starting to be a real pro after having treated such an incredible number of wounded. I had become attached to some of them for all sorts of reasons. I knew the time would come when I wouldn't have the choice to leave this place, and I was anticipating the pain I would feel at abandoning them to their sad fate. Two months went by without changing our way of doing things. There were, of course, small disagreements between my sisters and I that brought us closer once we had gotten over them. We quite often raised each other's morale when things were not going as we hoped. The first year was ending and things were changing in a way such that we no longer knew what tomorrow would hold for us. Sometimes, I just wanted to curl up into a ball and get on the first flight back to Percé without looking back so that I could hold my family against my heart.

Getting in touch with other countries had become a luxury that no one could access easily. Life had become cruel, and we created this cruelty by pitting nation against nation for no logical reason. I saw only hatred and misery throughout this journey, and God no longer existed in the hearts of anyone. The six months went by and gave way to another month of Christmas even worse than the previous ones. I could only think that this Christmas was becoming like those that I fled when I still had nothing. There was always this malicious aspect in nature that reminded me again how much my childhood memories had disturbed me. The worst years were the ones when I had never been able to reunite my little sisters, my older brothers and my mother for the holidays. But this one deprived me of the family I had finally been able to create with my flesh and blood and family that existed only painfully in my memories. On the night of December 24th, 2030, when I expected it the least, the Commander of Egypt visited us, taking the trouble to bring some very essential gifts, especially for us, the women. He confirmed that the rumours about us that had been spreading over the past few months were real. He was more than surprised to hear that we were providing considerable assistance, day after day, to soldiers who did not belong to our country of origin. We used the provisions he had brought us to put together a small, ordinary Christmas party. The party brightened every heart that was suffering and above all, brought new hope for a better tomorrow. I think that this year gave me a little personal satisfaction despite my inner suffering from not being able to spend the holidays with my family. We were able to bring a lot of peace, compassion and love to all those who really needed it. I had not touched alcohol for years, but I accepted, on the insistence of the Commander, his little glass of cognac. I was happy to see him in better shape with a more upbeat spirit in these times of celebration. He couldn't believe how my sister and I resembled each other. He did not forget to comment that Jack was luckier than he was to have had me as a wife. After a long pause, he turned to finally promise me that he would do everything in his power to have a plane help us leave Jerusalem. I couldn't have expected anything better from him, and I hastened to show my gratitude. Even in these times of celebration, he had to take leave of us to return to his base. He looked at me, sorry to have to fulfill his obligations in such an occasion, and shortly afterward, he left us. In our eighth month, two months after Christmas, we were out getting some fresh air with death on our minds; it seemed a few of us were starting to lose hope when I analyzed some of their reactions. Deborah faced me and looked at the sky with a sudden expression of contentment, as if she knew that we would leave soon. It wasn't long before the plane that she contemplated in the distance landed a few blocks from where we were staying. Our chance to leave that place had finally come, and I knew it. They came and announced our happy departure to us not long after landing. I thought that when I'd see that day, I would jump for joy, kissing everyone and asking them to hurry, then we would board the plane as fast as possible and it would be nothing more for us than a simple, distant memory. Unfortunately, just the opposite happened, and my heart broke into a thousand pieces. I couldn't get on the plane and leave those poor people to bear so much misfortune. They understood our commitment and did not hurry us to leave. They wished that we would change our minds and stay with them forever. We eventually said our farewells to most of the wounded we had treated. They seemed to be much better than before. I got used to the idea that my adventure was just beginning. Somehow, I managed to keep my composure and not burst into tears. I saw that my sisters, once they had boarded the plane, were doing much better. The relationship between Peter and my brother had developed because they were quickly taken with one another. Since the first week in Israel, they had bonded in a sincere friendship. They only separated to sleep and took pleasure in working as a team. I had difficulty imagining them no longer being together in the future. Their sudden brotherly love was a joy to see. The Apostle Isaac and Pastor Osteen also developed a very powerful connection. We women became the protected ones of the whole gang. Badouri's wife and I had never been very close, but the mission brought us closer in an incredible way. I noticed how shy she was. It was a stopover that did not lack for praise. We quickly took off without anyone offering to leave with us.

After an eight-hour layover in Al Furat, which we thought we would never leave, we landed in Baghdad two days later. At first, in the Al Furat airport, they suspected us because they spoke neither French nor English. But Deborah, who was cleverer than we were, showed them hundreds of photos, which were proof that we were considered orderlies in other countries. They no longer asked us about the reason behind our trip across the entire continent, and after making sure that we didn't have any dangerous weapons, they wished us good luck. I don't know how long I slept, but as soon as I lay my head against the backrest in the plane to Baghdad, I fell into a virtual coma until we landed. I had a strange dream in which I saw myself being chased by legendary creatures, giant men called "Bigfoot." They had managed to capture us and took pleasure in being served as if we had become their slaves. I woke with a start because my dream seemed a little too real. Opening my eyes, I had a bad feeling that did not leave me for hours without really being able to explain it. The entire crew smiled at me normally but couldn't understand how I felt after having such a nightmare. I couldn't keep it to myself. I absolutely had to tell my sisters about it. I said to myself that we would be a little more aware of what could possibly happen. I took them away from the questioning looks of my friends and told them about what I could see during my dream. Jenny, alerted by the same feeling, asked me to share it with the others. I lost no time following her advice, and advising them to be cautious, I informed them about what I had seen. We had confidence in God, but we were also keenly aware that the devil had his eye on us. We knew that he would persecute us until we lost ourselves in this battle. We became disciples whose cause could not be compared to any kind of earthly wealth. Once in Baghdad, for safety reasons, we followed patrollers in a large secured stronghold to cooperate as best we could and answer certain routine questions. Three hours elapsed, and we were still being retained. At the end of four hours, we met the great-grandson of one of the most ancient princes of Iran, deceased since February 11th, 1979, known formerly under the name of Ali-Reza Pahlavi. He was one of the high-ranking officers. At first, we didn't know who we were dealing with since he was dressed in simple clothes and was not haughty or unkind to us. On the contrary, he spoke with us very courteously and understandingly. As I studied his slightest movements, I felt he exuded a certain class and a lot more power than the other officers. His confidence and attractiveness belied his false modesty, and I realized after a few minutes he only had eyes for Deborah. His French and even his English were much too perfect to be just anyone's grandson. He was not embarrassed and even seemed comfortable making all sorts of jokes to my sister. I saw things that others could not yet realize, and I ended up becoming aware that the other armed men always had an eye on him but never dared interrupt him in any way. I understood much later, when we went with him, the reason that had caused him to come help us. Five hours after our encounter with the famous Prince Ali-RahPah Mohammad, we were invited to fly with him on his private plane. I had no confidence in this man, and I saw that women were not considered equals. I would have gladly declined this invitation that I considered more an order than anything else. It seemed that he expected that we be grateful to have been spared from prison and received as guests of honour to travel next to a prince. I don't think that a refusal on our part to board that plane would have been tolerated, all the more so because he was always throwing murderous glances at Obama, as if to show the hatred he felt. The Apostle Isaac, who had finally woken up, and who did not want to see us separated, replied positively in a more diplomatic manner, while shaking his hand to end all suspicions. When we landed in Iran, a dozen armoured trucks in the service of the prince awaited his arrival to take their positions. The man we had come to know in Baghdad soon turned into another severe, less friendly man. He saw nothing in us but men and women who could hurt him in the future. Once in the open air, he turned toward the men of the mission, asking: "All those who are not with me are against me. So, gentlemen, which one of you would be brave enough to fight by my side today?" I knew that I had no right to speak because he completely ignored us. Only Deborah had been able to find favour in his eyes, as if he was showing her that he would do anything for her to accept him. I couldn't let any of the men fall into his trap and risk being executed. I approached and replied to him in a courageous and sensible manner with these words: "Mr. Mohammad, I'm sure that according to your ideology, your war is probably the best, but if we decide to join it, it will automatically mean that we deny our God. However, we have made a great journey not to make war, but to regain the balance. You seem to be an experienced, intelligent man capable of recognizing the difference between men of laws and men of faith. We are part of the second category because we are men and women sent to prevent this world from disappearing and taking with all life with it. Today, know that these men are placed under my protection. Yes, under a woman. Now you are left with two choices: either you let us go while joining us to win the good fight, or you let us go and you continue to fight, causing your death and the death of your people. In both cases, you will act wisely, but I guarantee you, the first way is the best one."

"Shut up, you arrogant woman," he shouted.

I wanted to keep talking, but he left me no other choice than to be quiet. I knew that I had spoken firmly and respectfully, but I didn't know if a woman had ever spoken to him that way. He approached me and slapped so hard that blood trickled from my nose. The others wanted to come to my assistance, but the soldiers pointed large machine guns at them and roughly turned them away. Deborah, who hadn't said anything until then, spoke very loudly and stood in front of me, looking at him defiantly. She understood that she really shouldn't stand up to this man. He resumed his speech, again addressing the men of God:

"I see that there are no men here, so every one of you will be locked up until you beg me to let you fight by my side." "And you," he said looking at me, "the only reason why I didn't cut your tongue out is your lovely sister, who is a rare gem that I'm seriously starting to like. But if you dare resist my orders, I'll throw you in jail like those bums. Now we're leaving."

They had us board trucks, and we passed through an Iranian city that was devastated all the way to our destination. Once we arrived, he ordered his bodyguards to imprison all those who did not change their minds. As for us, since he was in love with one of the four sisters, whom he said would inevitably soon become his new conquest, he kept us with him on the condition of serving him night and day without any form of rebellion. He categorically refused to take Élizabeth, Badouri's wife Julie or their daughters, even when my sister got down on her knees and begged him to spare them. His private apartments were located five layers below the ground. Underneath the tunnel, which before the war had been called the Tohid Tunnel, and no one approached within ten metres of it without being shot. His housing was worthy of a man of his rank.

Unfortunately, we weren't the only women to have been brought for the same reasons. There were around a hundred of them of different colours, races and ages, each one more beautiful than the last. I could describe this place as being the secret harem of Prince Mohammad.

We had been forced to follow a man as egotistical as he was. He had underestimated the greatness of our mission and, without a second thought, imprisoned innocent men who refused to embrace his cause. What he had not yet realized was not just limited to us but to the suffering of each of the women he kept prisoner for his personal satisfaction.

In my opinion, I think that God had heard the tears and prayers of those young women, who couldn't leave the prison and lead a normal life. Our mission took yet another twist that didn't please me at all. I shivered whenever I thought about it again. The only question I constantly asked myself was how to get out of this place alive and at the same time, rescue everyone who wanted to escape. Deborah flatly refused to share the room offered to her by the prince. She begged him to be patient with the woman he said he desired. He had no choice but to accept her request. He even seemed aroused at having been turned down and imagined that she would eventually come around.

He wished her to beg him to take her back because, on his orders, we could only move from one room to another inside the prison. They placed us together in a large room that looked much more like a cell in an orphanage than anything else. My first night made me think about the years when

I was a mere cabaret dancer. Some of these women smiled at us in welcome. The ones who thought that they had really belonged to the prince for a long time looked us over with much more jealousy. Their eyes said everything about all the misery that we would have experienced if there had not been four of us entering that place.

Years in bars had led me to be cautious about trusting other women. With their jealousy, you could never be too sure what they were capable of. Sometimes I wanted to be part of certain cliques, make friends with them and confide in some of them, but I was always afraid of being betrayed. They could easily have reported me to the police if things weren't going like they wanted them to. Most of these young women had to go through all sorts of major problems to continue evolving in such a sketchy environment, and I had often reminded myself of that fact. I was always the one who didn't ever fit in any group, and especially the one who had more enemies because, for a black woman, I attracted too much attention. There were some who nevertheless tried to intimidate me but without much success. Today, when I think about it, I know that angels were always there protecting me in each of the various situations I've lived through. God is faithful, yesterday, today and tomorrow, and I thank him that things happened that way. The new phase between concrete walls reminded me of this yet again, except that now I had stopped being afraid.

I told my little sisters to be careful. We lost no time in starting our prayers and forming our famous circle where we joined hands. To get out of this hell, we knew we seriously needed the hand of God. We wanted to understand the reason why we were there. After our first prayer, the women understood the reason we had been sent inside that place and automatically approached us. They wanted to tell us something about themselves, but we couldn't understand the languages they spoke. Each used a different dialect and this new problem prevented us from understanding the reality of the situation. Our arrival raised all those who did not accept us against those who were coming closer and closer to be able to talk to us. For some of them we had become a major threat. I was thinking that we had to proceed with caution without alarming the soldiers. Every day that passed, we brought in a different woman. None of the forty first women we questioned spoke our languages. Among them, there women from many nations: Russia, Iran, Lebanon, Ukraine, Poland, Germany, Spain, Romania, Syria,

India, Ethiopia, Palestine, Ireland, Iraq, Panama, Colombia, Peru, El Salvador, Egypt, Portugal, and Brazil. There were a few from each small town of the Mediterranean lands and islands to the east and the west; there were women from almost all the world's countries, each more beautiful than the last, each with unique personalities. The prince was what I would describe as a collector of beauties. I realized that he had them all taken at a young age, and now he was going after us to complete his collection. I wondered how he could exploit other people so brazenly. When the Egyptian woman arrived, we were happy to see that she spoke French as well as we did. I had a lot of questions, and I didn't know where to start. She entered peacefully, and her first reaction was to hug all four of us without worrying about what the others would say.

"We should be very discreet," I began by telling her.

She looked at each of us in turn, and said, "You all look the same, it's amazing!"

I didn't know about what my sisters thought, but I could already guess the young woman's age. I decided to ask her anyway, "How old are you?"

"I'm not too sure, but I think I'm nineteen years old."

"What's your name, and where are you from?" asked Jenny.

"I'm from Egypt, and my name is Cybile."

"Since when have you lived here?" asked Deb.

"My whole life. I came here when I was six."

"Oh my God!" exclaimed Lindsay.

"Is that the case for all the others too?" I asked.

"Yes, we all came here when we were very young."

"You have all shared that man's bed?" asked Lindsay tearfully.

"Yes," she timidly answered. "When he goes on a trip, the men responsible for watching over us also take the liberty of coming to our beds. They threaten to kill us if we talk about what they make us suffer."

I couldn't believe it. At that moment, I finally understood the gravity of the situation.

"Do you talk with other women here, Cybile? "Are you friends?" asked Jenny.

"We don't all understand each other because of our languages differences, but we have created a dialect that helps us understand a modicum of what we want to say to each other. There are a few great girls here, you know. I love them very much. We often pray together. Very often, we don't know what to say. We don't understand why we do it. Maybe because we cry a lot, and we are very afraid, but we try to do it whenever we can. How about you? Why are you here? We have all seen that you're not embarrassed to do what we were doing in secret," she eventually admitted.

"Oh! You want to talk about praying!" Said Deb smilingly when she saw the young girl's confused face.

"We are here to free you, I replied seriously, looking her right in the eyes. Otherwise, I don't see why God would make us take this major detour. He has heard your cries and tears, and he wants you to know that you are not all alone in this world." "God?" asked the young woman without understanding the word's meaning.

"God is the most powerful of all beings in the world. He allows us to live, and it is He who acts when something is not going well to make the impossible become possible."

I knew that she couldn't understand what she had never known.

"When will your god help us get out of here?" she wanted to know.

Her question made me smile, and I replied:

"I don't know yet, but he will do it. If he made us come in here, he will get us out in due time. Above all, we should try to tell all those who wish to know the information that I have just shared with you. I won't be able to do it without your help, Cybile. My name is Melissa. Jenny is my younger sister, who is followed by my sister Lindsay. Deborah is the youngest, and my doppelgänger. She's the reason we're here."

After having met us, she left and promised to help as best she could in informing the others. I already saw that it would not be an easy task, and I thought that it was no longer my fight but God's. For this reason, I didn't worry too much. Two days later, the Prince ordered that my sister be brought to him. She was afraid, but she left with the conviction that nothing would happen with that man. When she came before him, I could feel the tension in the air. My sisters and I were on our knees fighting him in spirit, when, at the moment he approached Deb, we felt a missile explode in northern Iran and the earthquake that immediately followed. There was a power failure after the event, and the Prince had no choice but to postpone this much-anticipated encounter. I expected nothing more from the god that I had learned to love and adore. The very moment my sister reappeared in our cell, her first question was, "Mel! What was that?"

"That, my dear, was the beginning of the wrath of Elohim," was my only answer.

I was concerned about my brothers and sisters imprisoned in less comfortable rooms than our own. I was wondering how I could help them. We were in the good graces of the soldier who served us our meals. I had carefully kept my wedding ring because when I missed my husband, I took it out of hiding, and I put it back on my finger and so deeply cherished the good memories that my sisters had come to follow my example. The fourth day, the same soldier, who was coming by to give us food, looked at it covetously but without knowing how to go about stealing it from me. When I saw his eyes on the jewelry, I thought to myself that the chance to help my friends had finally come. Fortunately, the man spoke fluent English. I called him over, showing off my piece of jewelry to him before I went for it.

"I'm ready to give you my ring," I said, testing the waters.

"But I want to know whether my friends are doing okay."

At first, he looked at me with curiosity and then with a look of pity. He answered vaguely, "They're fine."

"How can I be sure of what you're telling me?"

"I don't always have the right to feed them," he replied forthrightly, but they aren't dead yet.

"I'll let you have this ring, which is worth $1.5 million, on one condition."

The words "millions of dollars" did not fall on deaf ears and his eyes widened. "Anything for you, your grace!" he exclaimed immediately.

"I want them to be fed regularly."

"But I don't have that right, and I'm being watched by others."

"I'm ready to give up my meal so that you can do what's needed. Just find a way to bring what I am asking you to them."

"I will do everything to satisfy your grace. And when will I be in possession of what you owe me?"

"In a few days, when you will have started your task. I want proof of what you are doing. Find something, some kind of evidence, anything."

"I'll do my best ma'am, he answered before walking away."

I expected nothing better of a soldier in that place. I placed no importance to a piece of jewelry that, in the end, wouldn't save us from our bad deeds. Pastor Hinn always kept a handkerchief, and, as evidence of the soldier's good faith, he gave it to him for a few days. My sisters and I gave up our meals half the time for our friends. I ended up parting with my wedding ring without feeling guilty, and the relief I felt in knowing that the others were eating their fill satisfied me even more. In the meantime, we were more than happy with the results obtained from the work that we were doing with the place's various young women. Many of them came to join us with Cybile in groups of two or three. The Prince was gone for several weeks, which gave us more time before he would become aware of what we were doing. We prayed with some, we consoled others, and we were hated by most of them despite our good will. I had known for a long time that we couldn't be accepted by everyone, but I felt sorry for all those who thought that their life consisted of living in a cell and sharing a man with a hundred other women.

I waited two months before finally venturing out with the soldier one evening to the rooms that were off limits to us. We had become more than people who were exchanging services. I had eventually won his respect and he, my trust. Despite his attempts to talk me out of it, I wouldn't be dissuaded. I followed him without even thinking about it because I had to make contact with the others. I found myself completely at the far end of my cell after a 15-minute walk in front of those men and women of God, who were in prayer. When they saw me, their surprise went straight to my heart. I kissed them through the bars, and I gave them a quick summary of the situation that we were experiencing in the other part of the tower of Mohammad. They then understand why we had been sent there. They thanked me for all the food I sent them through this good soldier and asked me to keep the faith. I couldn't stay any longer, and I had to return by the same route back to my cell. The next day, Jenny wanted to have her turn to go so that she could see her husband. The soldier was afraid and refused at first; he did not want to be executed and begged me not to ask such dangerous things of him.

My sister, desperate, also gave him her wedding ring. She knew the risk if they were caught, but she didn't care: her desire was beyond all reasoning. The soldier helped get her into contact with Dimitrova, and coming back from this adventure, he made it clear to us that he would no longer risk his life for us. From then on, he would limit himself to feeding us; otherwise, he would be happy to let someone else take his place. His help had become crucial in my eyes; for this reason, I couldn't risk losing him. I promised him not to force him to take such risks.

The Prince, back from his trip, once again tried to see my sister, except that this time, something gave him the scare of his life. According to Deb, the moment he laid his hands on her chest to caress it, his hands were burned to the third degree in only a few seconds. The soldiers, who were alerted immediately by his screams, quickly removed my sister on the Prince's orders. She was brought back 40 minutes later after being called all kinds of names, without being abused, lest they suffer the same fate as the Prince. This new situation caused us no small trouble since they redoubled their surveillance of us. According to my calendar, it was July 2031. Four months and one week had already passed, and we had no idea how much longer we would have to spend in that place. Sixty of the women were ready to leave with us. They barely understood how we operated but had decided to give it a shot. We had not taken the risk to make them understand that, outside, total chaos reigned. I could see in their eyes how they had had enough of being imprisoned for so long. Many of them had very strong personalities and could be very effective in convincing others who did not want to participate in the escape. The Prince summoned me a week after his bad experience with my sister. I could see that he was afraid of getting too close but was expecting that I provide an explanation to make him spare her life.

"Prince Ali," I began, "I could try to provide you with a thousand explanations for what happened in the room with my little sister, but the fact is that I'm not sure about any of them. I can simply tell you that without a doubt, it's plain to see that we serve a god different than yours. He merely warned you of what he can do if you try to keep us or even think about hurting us."

He laughed after my speech and left me no choice but to look at him in disbelief:

"I think you're losing your mind, my dear. Let me enlighten you a bit by admitting to you that the only reason you're still alive, you and your sisters, is because of your striking resemblance with my mother, you see, especially Deborah whose smile is exactly like hers. At first, I thought it remarkable, and then it became an obsession."

I wasn't at all reluctant to ask, "And all these poor girls you have locked away, do they remind you of your dear mother as much as we do?"

"Shut up. You have no right to speak. I'm the one who asks questions around here. Is that clear enough?"

Without paying attention to his rude remark, I continued, "You're a disgrace to your kind, and I pity you."

He took a step forward, and I took two to avoid him slapping me again. "Women have no right to speak in my home. And you are no exception to this rule, negress. Oh, by the way, I have nevertheless made the effort to read a few of your books. I really have to say that I tip my hat to you. I'll keep you here to write my story so that the whole world remembers me after I'm gone."

"You'll die in the shadows, and I'd rather die than to share my intellect with a man like you, Prince Ali."

His eyes grew stern as he heard me contradict him. I can guarantee you that I meant every word I spoke to that despicable person.

"Guard!" he shouted as he let the soldier enter who had been stationed behind the door. Please bring this viper back to her cell."

He turned to face me and added, "If you don't do what I ask, I'll execute you one after the other until your turn comes."

I couldn't believe it. I absolutely had to get out of this place. In moments like these, I blamed myself for taking this trip. I did not understand why God would put me to the test.

I told my sisters of the discussion I had with the Prince, and they begged me to accept until a better solution became available.

"We need to start praying!" I said, in tears. "I won't feel safe writing a story in his presence."

"Then ask him whether all four of us can be there together to assist you," suggested Lindsay.

"He would never want that, said Deborah. Not after what happened with me."

"Nothing ventured, nothing gained," said Jenny.

Two days later, he had them come to get me. I told myself that it was now or never to make my proposal to him, and I just asked him straight away, "I have thought about your request, and I will do it on one condition . . ."

"Ah yes!" he exclaimed, surprised.

"I would like my sisters to be with me so that I can be comfortable enough to produce something worthy of a prince."

"If I turn this request down, I imagine you'll also stay firm in your decision of not cooperating."

"I would have no other choice than to refuse, Prince Ali, and no matter what the consequences are."

I saw that he was mulling over my proposal, and, not knowing what we were up to, he sent me back to my cell and promised to give me an answer as soon as possible. I could see he didn't mind the idea of studying our four characters at the same time; in fact, his eyes shone with excitement. Two days later, his decision was made, and he sent two soldiers to get us. I was wondering what all this meant, and especially the reason that caused him to accept. It was a very positive sign that he required my talent as a writer. I had to use this to my advantage to help the others out of their cell, and I had a good idea about how to go about doing it.

We were playing the game of being pretty and answering him when he asked us questions. He began his story, and I wrote along with him. At first, he posted soldiers with us. But after a few days, when he realized that we were not dangerous, he eventually ordered them to stand guard outside. At no time did we neglect to say our prayers when arriving in the morning and before returning to our cell. I noticed his fascination with seeing us interact. He in no way objected to and even took pleasure in seeing us in action. Every day that passed, without him knowing it, gave us more access to his unconscious. I felt that the time would come when he would ask us the questions he had been keeping to himself until then.

It had been too long since I had been in contact with the others and I was very worried about them. Almost every night, Jenny cried her eyes out, imagining that her husband would not survive too long in such wretched conditions. At the beginning of September, when all four of us arrived in a bad mood, he realized very quickly that something was not going well. After our prayer, he asked us what was wrong. Without giving me time to answer, Jenny took the lead:

"What have the men, who were accompanying us some time ago, done to you, Prince Ali?" asked my sister, displaying her foul demeanour.

"Oh, she has decided to talk, this one," he said derisively. "Well, you can rejoice because I changed their location, my dear. In the last two months, their conditions have improved remarkably. And would you believe that

I even have participated in the same kind of prayers that you have been making me endure for some time."

"When will you let us go?" asked Deborah, who was speaking to him for the first time since the unfortunate event."

"As soon as your sister finishes my story, believe me, and not before!"

"We would like to see them."

"Why would I grant you such a favour?" he asked me, seeming bored.

"Because you can't stop my sister from seeing her husband, and us from seeing our brother and our friends."

"Her husband?" he exclaimed, surprised. "I never knew that . . . "

He paused to try to understand which of us was married.

"It's me," said Jenny.

"What a pretty picture! And when were you going to tell me this news? Which one of those men is the brother then? I have heard everything now."

"Tell me, Prince Ali, did you ask our permission to kidnap us? So, did you think that we trusted you enough to tell you about our private lives? That is the least of your worries right now. We know that what really interests you boils down to your pitiful story."

I continued in the same tone to make him see the reality of the situation.

"Outside, Prince Ali, it's war and chaos, the world is dying, and you, you think humans intelligent enough will remain who will worry about mundane stories like yours. Let me tell you that it will never happen because God will ensure that this story dies with its master. We will have to leave, and we will have to leave soon, and I would ask you to come with me if you could still use your brain! You will also have to let go all these poor, innocent girls who do not want to perish in this sinister place with you."

"Finally, you have decided to talk. I was wondering if the cat had gotten your tongues. I think we have talked too much for today, and, as a result, I would politely ask you to please return to your cells."

We got up to leave when he told me, "I don't think I asked you to leave," he said, staring at me with a look that I was unfamiliar with. The others may go but not you."

"What makes you think that I am still willing to continue helping you?"

"I would like to talk with you alone, please."

He had changed his tone. I softened, feeling that we had managed to touch enough sore points. I motioned to my sisters that I wished to stay so that they wouldn't worry about anything. Once alone, he opened up to me in an incredible way:

"You know, I'll let you go, but I want you to take my story so that the world remembers me, even when I'm gone. I've kept having the same dream for over a month. I see myself in my bed sleeping, and when I wake up, I'm fighting in vain against a very powerful, invisible hand. He grabs my throat so strongly that in the end I'm suffocating, and I die without being rescued by any of my soldiers. Once dead, I see you entering the room, you and others. You form a large circle around my bed. I can't open my eyes, but I'm conscious enough to realize that even after all I put you through, you are taking the time to pray for me. You ask your god to forgive me and accept me in his heaven. Without anyone being able to stop you, you manage to get out of my tower and, once you're gone, having taken all my women with you, everything inside begins to catch fire and the rest of my staff perishes with me. Nothing is left after you. The first time I had this dream, I thought maybe it was the fruit of my overactive imagination, but when it returned week after week, I took it as a warning. That is the reason why I asked you to write my story. I think I'm fighting against something more powerful than me, and I'm doomed if I don't let you go."

I was shocked to hear him say such a thing to me, and I then understood why he became more attentive to the prayers we said every time.

"I can finish your story within two to three days, I answered him. You still have the choice of coming with us.

"My place is here with my people in this war. But I thank you for your offer. I will leave you my private plane, and you will be able to go with all those who want to follow you.

I couldn't believe my ears; understanding the expression on my face, he smiled at me and reconfirmed it one last time:

"I give you my word that you will be able to leave as soon as you have finished that story.

"I can keep working on it right now, Prince Ali."

"No, please call me Ali."

I set to work, and I stopped to eat something quickly. I returned to my cell very late, and I found my sisters waiting for me and praying that I come back to them in one piece. The scene made me smile, and I lost no time in telling them everything. They shouted with joy and asked more than once if I believed him. I knew that God had acted, and the time had finally come for us to continue our mission. Two days later, he kept his word and freed the men of God before our departure. I jumped into the arms of each of my friends with infinite joy, forgetting my good manners. We had all lost quite a few kilos by not eating properly. I finished his story that night, and I promised to personally ensure that it became one of the best-known stories in the future. Even now, I remember that day as if it were yesterday. Years after the war, I fought with the new system to produce this man's story. Today, he is recognized as one of the heroes of the 23rd century of Chin Lee because of his courage for having released us so that we could continue our journey.

We left as soon as possible on the most beautiful, luxurious plane, which we had never seen before, with fifty of the women, who had willingly and mentally prepared for their lives to be radically changed. Everything in the interior was made of purely carved gold. We flew over the other continents to Nepal without having unpleasant surprises anywhere else. Once we arrived, we had no choice but to continue on alone to find the waterfall. To do this, we first had to go to Tibet through Nepal's still intact forests. I realized that the women had never experienced the outside world since their earliest youth. They could not control their excitement and spoke incessantly. I prayed that no unfortunate event would happen again, because for the moment, there were too many of us. I was wondering what God was going to do with all these women who each represented very different countries. I realized that his plan was always extraordinary and unpredictable. I'm sure that others faced the same questions as I did, except that they didn't ask them out loud. Nepal was virtually the only place that the bombs had not yet destroyed. Once in the heart of the forest, after three long days, we stopped to rest when, suddenly, we felt tremors that made the surface of the earth vibrate. We gathered together as the tremors approached us. It took a good five minutes to understand that instead of an earthquake, we were dealing with bigfoot. They looked just as they did in my dream. I realized that I had experienced a premonition that we weren't able to prevent. There were many of them, and we seemed tiny in comparison. I was looking at King Kong surrounded by his whole family. They surrounded us, and I saw the end coming . . . I couldn't imagine a more terrible death than to be eaten by giant monkeys.

Since they were wild animals, I was surprised to find that they distinguished between women and men. I was already picturing our trip on their shoulders once we would make friends with them. Thank God, most of us were women; the contrary would have simply resulted in a huge disaster.

They were gentle and kind with us but changed their demeanor with the men, as if they felt competition from them. I quickly found one of them who was enamoured with me whom I called George. He put me on his shoulder, and we began to play together. The others, spurred on by their animal curiosity and spirit of competition, also found themselves one and even several women so they could do the same. We just had to think of a way of convincing them to help us continue our journey. I knew that I would not be able to do so without help from above. They were, however, animals who were devoid of any ability to communicate.

I had to be sure that I could count on George's devotion. I was concerned about the reason that these animals had magically appeared before us. We had thought before that day that bigfoot were purely legendary. I finally had the idea to draw a map representing the waterfall, one that was large enough to make them understand where we wanted to go. After several non-verbal signs, they rose up and began to make gestures, beating their big hairy hands on their chests. As for George, he followed me everywhere, which gave me courage for my future quest. Our first attempt to encourage them to leave with us fell totally flat, to the point that Pastor Lucado had advised us to give up and continue on without them. I was not too sure I wanted to give up on my project, but I didn't want to delay the others, who did not share my ability to see impossible things happening. We decided to give up and start off, leaving our friends behind us. It did not take too long for them to realize that we were raising anchor, and three of them followed, leaving their own kind behind. I didn't know if it was Georges or another one,

but, when he drew closer as he looked for me, I felt that my efforts had not been in vain. The others, who had stayed behind, immediately embarked on the adventure with them. This is how the last stretch of our voyage to Tibet took place, on the backs of about 20 bigfoot . . .

I shared Georges with my sisters as well as Ouraha, an Iranian, and Marchiela, a Swede, whom we had come to love from the very beginning. They were both very young and reminded me all the time of one of my grandnieces whom I haven't yet told you about in this story. They were funny and displayed such innocence that I routinely forgot their painful life experiences. Late September was approaching, and we were happy to have found these animals to overcome the beginnings of cold weather. We were progressing so fast in the first three days that we were forced to stop and let our friends, who almost no longer wanted to move, rest. It was a day of recuperation for all of us. I was always the first to motivate the crew.

I was filling the role as the group nag, but we were close to the end of our trip, and I wanted to finish it as quickly as possible. I was wondering why the trip would last six years since we had almost arrived at our destination. Mimi was the Chinese girl who never spoke, but when she wanted to express herself, everybody was quiet and automatically turned their attention to her. This gesture always ended up making her uncomfortable, and sometimes she didn't even finish her sentences. I asked myself a lot of questions about each of these girls, and each time, I emerged from my reflections increasingly confused.

Since they were with us, I knew they would no doubt be part of the story, but what role they would play once they arrived there remained a total mystery to me. We resumed our voyage through the jungle and, after ten days, with giant strides, we arrived west of the waterfall of the Himalayas.

Now you should understand that we had finally arrived at our destination. The only person we sent out ahead of this scene was my brother-in-law Dimitrova. Not because we were afraid but because the trip had started because of his dream. He mustered all his courage and advanced until he had no choice but to stop in front of the waterfall. I was expecting that everything would happen very quickly since we had finally arrived there, except that nothing happened as planned. There was no one to greet us as heroes, even when we tried, each in turn, to appear before the waterfall, just as Dimi had.

"Wait!" Pastor Osteen said. "Can anyone explain this to me? Is all this part of the trip?"

"We should simply be patient," added Pastor Hinn in his role as the wise elder."

"From the beginning, said Mr. Sarkozy, losing his temper. "we have sacrificed everything we had. How much time do we still have before perishing as we go back the way we came?"

My brother, who was always the first to lose his temper, kept quiet for once. I could hear everyone heedlessly arguing for several minutes; I sensed that something in the atmosphere prevented us from seeing clearly. I would have said that an evil force had taken hold of some of us. I understood that we had come much too close to just drop everything and retrace our steps as some were strongly urging. My sisters, who had not heard me utter a single word since the beginning of the scene, moved closer to me.

"What should we do Mel," Lindsay said to me quietly. "They're practically killing each other. Shouldn't we do something?"

I knew that my sister was right, but I felt weak. It seemed like all my energy was being sapped. Without understanding what was happening, I touched the hand of my bigfoot, and we entered into what I would describe as a fusion of our minds. I could talk to him through my thoughts since I could perfectly hear his.

The incredible was happening. Through his mouth, I screamed so loudly that the depths of the earth still remember that moment. There was a silence, and I spoke through his lips before fainting.

"Don't be afraid it's me Mel. I don't know what is happening or how I can control this animal, but I must speak to you because time grows short, and I feel very weak. A force that we can't control lives in this place. The only way to fight it is unity and a great, heartfelt prayer. Time is running out, and we must hurry. The longer we remain in darkness, the more we prove to the creator that we are not worthy of fulfilling the promise. Something is keeping me from breathing . . . "

I couldn't finish my sentence, and I passed out. My mind had left the bigfoot, who was not conscious either because, like me, he fell to the ground completely unconscious.

Something extraordinary happened once my body stopped working. My soul left my inert body on the ground and then took on another, completely different life. Not only was I able to see the humans, but I could also perceive what was not visible to the eye. Two Seraphim were placed at the end of the waterfall but could not intervene to help us because of the beast. Yes, a three-headed beast had surrounded us but was not allowed to attack us since, each time, it rammed into an invisible wall. I was between life and death, the world that I visited was a world that no human left without divine assistance. When the beast saw me, it turned away from my friends and started approaching me. The only thing I was able to do was to shout, "Father! Have mercy upon your servant."

At that moment, I saw Dimitrova, impelled by his instinct, move closer to the waterfall. Once in front of it, he didn't realize that he was face to face with the seraphim placed before it. These heavenly angels couldn't let us see them, our eyes could not have withstood such a spectacle. They were colossal, and they had six wings. Their faces were hidden at all times by the first two wings and their hands were placed in each of the wings in the middle. I thought I was dreaming, but I was the only one to see such an uncanny spectacle. I cried out with all my strength to Dimitrova to be able to spiritually whisper to him what his eyes could not understand. I knew that he had heard when he instinctively put his hand inside the waterfall in the middle of the two seraphim, who, like me, contemplated the scene without intervening.

I imagine that they had received orders. It was our fight not theirs, and it was up to us to find the solution. Dimitrova was able to automatically set off the process of the mechanism of going from our world to the new one. He was the only one among us during all this time who emitted a retroactive energy able to transcend time. The beast became more and more enraged and came so close to me that I thought that I wasn't going to be able to cross back over to my world. It was two centimetres away when I saw an intense light streaming from the waterfall that deprived me of sight. I became blind at that moment.

I couldn't be dead because I was still able to think; my eyes had seen too many things that I was not ready to understand. This was the last sacrifices that I gave to the future world as I became one of its founding mothers. The door opened for my friends, who had long since knelt to worship the God who did not wish to see us all perish. I came to and no one understood what had happened to me before realizing what I had lost. My other senses, such as my hearing and touch, developed instantly. Sometime later, I developed a strong vision that enabled me to see events before they occurred.

You might think that the story ended at the waterfall, but this was not the case. We managed to open the door, but it took us two more years and one month to explore the place. I must explain this to you more clearly. The path was like nothing that we had previously known on earth. We thought in the beginning that we had spent only a few days, but we were completely wrong. We had arrived with 66 people and we had inherited a completely new world. We had received a second chance at dwelling with living species whose existence you are not yet unaware of, such as giant eagles, centaurs, winged horses, different kinds of dinosaurs that disappeared long before humans appeared on planet earth and trees whose roots were comparable to human brains. We were back in communication with all these species. This was the only time that we heard the voices that came from the depths of heaven, and we all fell flat on our stomachs because we couldn't do otherwise.

"I gave you one more chance because you demonstrated great determination that I saw nowhere else. You have travelled four years and one month to reach the last secret place. You need to go back to rescue the others, who are dying where you left them. You will cross over more quickly with the giant eagles whom I will ask to heed your wishes for a period of one year and one month. Of the six years given to you, you still have another year and a month that won't end until the moment when you again return here accompanied by the others. You will be able to bring with you each of your families, and you will return here in order to resume the same journey because, in exactly two years and two months, what you found here will be completely destroyed. Other Eagles will follow you for all who will believe in you and will want to follow you. Don't look back when you're returning, otherwise you will perish with the old creation. I'll have my eye on you. One last thing: thanks for keeping the faith. Each of these women you have rescued has no other family; that is why they will become a different nation unto themselves. Melissa, do you have a specific question to ask me?"

"Yes, Lord," I answered, overcome with emotion. "Why can I not regain my sight?"

"Because I can't erase what you have already seen from your memory. For this, you will become the mother of the new homeland. You will act with wisdom and goodness. Now go in peace, my children."

Only twelve returned with me on the quest for the family members. We flew over all the countries that we had previously crossed, and we came as expected to the island of Percé. For some of us, we found a few family members who had been spared by the war. I found my little girls but neither Jack nor my mother. I didn't know what to think of this new situation when my Eagle spoke to me.

"Don't cry, mother of nations, you will dream of them again. They have been brave."

It was at that point that I knew they were dead. I was anxiously watching everyone because I knew that time was running out before total destruction. After a short speech, I read the panic and confusion in everyone's eyes. I knew that there was very little hope to successfully convince everyone to leave with us. Time was running out, and we couldn't force anyone to change their minds about staying. It's at that point that I heard his voice. "Mel," he said as if we had just seen each other the day before.

I couldn't see him, but I knew he was watching me.

"Vano," I answered in a tentative tone. "We absolutely must leave now; otherwise, we will die here with this creation. Another world awaits us, you have to come with me now."

He did not hesitate a second, and he climbed onto the back of my eagle, which I was already sharing with my girls. For me, it was an emotional day that I couldn't explain. Shortly afterward, we left as quickly as we had come. It took sixty-six people to reach the Garden of Eden to enable many others to have the opportunity to enter. Six hundred and sixty-six people contributed to the advancement of humanity. When the world was destroyed, and there were too many of us to stay inside the garden, we all agreed to go back outside. We began to build roads and a floating infrastructure. We were using a new artificial intelligence software capable of running everything. There was no government, but a new socialist society that freely provided for all our needs. Our system, which had become the system of Chin Lee, ran everything. In no time, we found enough energy, and we were able to move our floating towns to different places. We created remedies that extended our youth. There were still not enough of us, but we were able to build a world that would become strong and structured enough to prevent any form of revolution against this new system.

Often, before falling asleep at night, I think about my past life during the years before the war. I can still see the flaw, but I try to understand the beginning of the revolution, wondering why it took place. And the truth is that, despite my memories and my old demons, who were part of me, I could not change what was no more. Tonight, sleep eludes me, and everything I can think about relates to the beginning of the revolution.

# CHAPTER 2

# *The Beginning of the Revolution*

WHEN ALL THIS STARTED, I was only thirty-seven years old. To tell you frankly, it had been years since the end of President Obama's term, which I had been dreading, because deep down I always knew that it would eventually happen. The years of war were the beginning of the extermination of the cities, I don't entirely know where, and it lasted thirteen long years. Donald Trump came to power at the end of Obama's presidency on January 20th, 2017. Things began to turn sour in the third month in March 2017. He had never really hidden his true nature and for that some fanatics adored him even more. It was only when he was re-elected that the last revolution inside the United States began. Trump was a vain and selfish being who was able to manipulate the Americans into rising against one another. He dismissed all those who stood in his way. Dividing to better rule, his new slogan, was just a strategy to achieve his ends. I had the chance to shake hands with him like the humblest of mortals and hear him talk more than once. He was simply a man filled with anger; his politics had brought no improvement. He was a true narrow-minded Republican who saw only his own best interests in absolutely everything. One of the last times we crossed paths, he really got on my nerves at a large charity gala organized by Unicef that I had invested a lot in so that it would be a success. I had been married for almost three years and the entire planet seemed to be aware of my marriage, except him. The situation in no way prevented him from making all kinds of bad jokes, as if were allowed to do anything . . . Personally, I had noticed on several occasions that he was never accompanied by his lovely wife Melania, and I told myself that the couple probably had their own reasons. After all, my husband left me free to travel without him and take care of different humanitarian projects around the world. In addition to the Americans, other people around the world had long noticed the various problems between the head of State and his wife.

The president partied a lot and attended just about any social event organized by Hollywood without worrying about what anyone would think of him and his behaviour. It was in this context that the last time we saw each other was September 28th, 2022, a year after the Unicef gala, just after his re-election to power. That evening, which could not have been more ordinary, was offered in homage to those who belonged to high society and had long since disappeared. I still remember the will power I needed to force myself to go there because it was the kind of evening that disgusted me. By pure principle, I had to represent my husband, G. J. Benjamin, who was bedridden due to an ill-timed fever. I had barely left and already regretted my decision; I felt sad to be so far from home. We had both simultaneously fallen under the spell of a lovely house built in Cape Code by an English duchess in 1999. We had barely had time to move when Jack had caught a bad flu. I had flown in his place, and I was starting to freak out for sorts of reasons.

Parties like these made me uncomfortable because I always considered myself an upstart. I may have had all those millions of dollars, but I never let it get to my head.

Barely out of the elevator, I met the President, accompanied by a veritable army that protected all his doings. As soon as he saw me, conversation ensued. I had to be polite and smile at him even though I knew his game. He was looking at me and, sometimes, staring at my chest as if I were a mere sex object in his eyes. I had chosen a magnificent red cocktail dress that was very long and very much in vogue that year. As the conversation became uncontrollable and persistent, I wanted to pick up and run away. I couldn't interrupt him by asking him for news of his wife for fear of angering him. Since the beginning of his first term, the entire world had compared him to the former tyrant Hitler. His eyes said it all about his intentions when he met a woman who interested him, and unfortunately, I had not gone unnoticed to him. I can tell you that I was more afraid than you think of this man and his murderous gaze. How can you put a stop to a conversation with such a powerful head of state when he believes that what he says is much more important than anything else? I felt nothing for him but a deep sadness, knowing that he held the fate of an entire population in his hands. I saw his real face and my blood froze. Yes, I was a celebrity, but this man had as much power as Hitler himself in his day, and remember what I told you about power.

It was unacceptable to organize this kind of evening while I was watching in the media so many children starve all over the world. I couldn't help all of them despite my involvement in many organizations. With so much money so badly invested in evenings like those, I could feel an evil spirit in the atmosphere; it seemed that the end was coming at such a pace that nothing seemed to work normally anymore. For a long time, I had been preparing, with all my interventions, to win the presidential elections of my own homeland, and my heart told me that I would do it. My husband sometimes discouraged me, but he knew how important to me it was to help the people that everyone pitied. The United States, during that same period, was doing very badly economically. Everything we saw indicated that something big would soon happen. I remember having repeated it to Jack several times; an unusual change would soon happen, but he did not take me seriously. I didn't wait until the end of that notorious evening to get out of there; I was out of place with this crowd of unaware people who were acting as if the rest of the world didn't exist. The ball had barely begun when I pretended to have a severe migraine. I apologized for my husband's absence. I managed to quickly bid farewell to some acquaintances who had worked with me at the beginning of my career. I knew I didn't want to linger in such a place that was more repugnant to me than anything. Immediately, after a short speech—I had won a prize for one of my books—I went to rejoin my husband and our twins.

During the second year of Trump's second term, there was more than one attack coming from all sides. The Americans began to revolt against their president, which had never happened before. This provoked a coup on March 20th, 2023. That's when the new Vice President, the totally unprepared Hillary Price, became president on March 30th, 2023, at 4:00 p.m. The relationship between the United States and Russia deteriorated during Price's term.

It was thus that the President, not knowing how to deal with the threats launched by other countries unhappy to see a woman at the head of the United States, plunged the world into total chaos after twenty-six months. The entire media said that Price was incapable of maintaining the United States in a state of peace. I am sure that all this had to happen in the end, and nobody was able to understand the magnitude of the events that occurred during and after the war because the reason for all that chaos was just inexplicable.

In my case, I was already a fast-rising success; my books had begun to make their way. I had signed my first book with the Éditions Vérone in Paris after two and a half years of waiting on March 3rd, 2017. That book was a debate-provoking sensation the moment it was published at the end of that same year. In the previous six years, I had become one a rarity: the most famous young black women of my time in the literary world, and it all had happened in no time. I had, for my own pleasure, worked on more than five films from my nineteen books.

I was living happily and seeing my dreams finally come true. Seven years of success had wonderfully passed, and I was finally happy to contribute to many projects that I had cared deeply about for a long time. In record time, my books had for the most part become legendary during that period, according to the New York Times. In September 2018, fortune had smiled at me, and I appeared on Oprah's show with my three little sisters. I had moved heaven and Earth to have them at my side.

The third part of My Precious will tell you about my youth in more detail and what pushed me toward writing, which became my only passion. All this had not taken too long because, just before retiring, Ellen DeGeneres also sent me an invitation to participate in her show. I appeared there, and it was a real success that propelled me into the film industry. I had fully dedicated myself to writing and released my third book four months after My Precious. The Twentieth Century Duke was also a success and then came my children's tale The Adventures of Orphilya, which charmed many readers. I had started to gain, beginning that first year, writing experience because I hadn't stopped since then.

I didn't take too long in releasing my four other great works, the rest of The Legend of the Soul Sisters. After publishing The Adventures of Orphilya, I had contract offers from many company executives until the day I finally decided to approach the man who made my heart race for the last time, which I thought I would never see happen. I did not hesitate one second in accepting the offer from the company that Jack had become the sole proprietor of. We know that only God and some good sorcerers can predict the future. I am neither one nor the other, but, nevertheless, I saw a future coming in which I evolved at light speed. Most of the time, certain obstacles make it so that we can't see occurrences created to move us forward, but even if we don't see them, we can still feel them approaching . . . This is simply called the universe, which gives us such a strong feeling that it allows us to feel our destiny coming . . .

I took great pleasure in working on three of my books with the man who was about to become, one year after our meeting in April 2020, my husband until this very day. I saw the sincerity in Jack's eyes, and I had hope for a better future. He was one among many others asking me to sign, but in an unconditional and inexplicable way, I had known for a long time that I was linked to that man. I had come a long way before that day, and I was finally ready, for all sorts of reasons, to jump into an adventure with him. He won my trust in a very short time and knowing he had always evolved in the world that I was just discovering made me feel tiny whenever he laid his eyes on me. Not long before, I had become a Christian again, and I had not shared a bed with any other man for over a year. He found many ways to break the ice between us through his kindness and attentiveness. He had become my mentor and best friend; we could laugh for hours without ever getting tired of talking to each other. He consoled me more than once when everything was going badly. I prayed to God that he accept the man who had already silently conquered my heart and one day he decided to follow me in becoming a Christian. I sincerely believe that he did so only to please me. From the beginning of our association in the film industry, our names also soon became legendary. Not long after that, he became a Christian and asked me to marry him. I was thirty-one years old at the time.

For most of us, it's a huge emotional shock to get out of our comfort zone. I wasn't born rich, I became rich thanks to my faith in a better future. When everything was going wrong, I turned to God desperately seeking to know the purpose of my presence on Earth. All I was aware of was my sublime internal and external beauty, but it didn't change anything when I considered my situation. I found myself even poorer than before, and the suffering I felt at not being able to have even the least bit of other people's wealth was slowly killing me day after day. I made sacrifices to God but only with the aim of attracting his gaze because, for me, he was the one who could answer my questions, not a man. After the sacrifices during my twenty-fifth summer, he answered me as clearly as I am talking to you right now. At that time, I knew that everything would change and that my life would never be the same. I knew that because of my background, I would bring a generational change to this world, and that the thousands of lives who would be in contact with me through my written knowledge and would identify me as a good example to follow.

My external beauty had often attracted as many problems as favours. For most of these problems, I was always able to get out of them in quite miraculous ways. This created my faith in the universe because the more I saw a miraculous hand acting on my most trifling problems, the more I began to believe a little more and think that he was perhaps really there watching over me. I always did the best I could, relying on myself and living the life I led since adolescence. I had one master: money. I left all the good values that my mother taught me by the wayside. Some days, I loved myself less when I looked in the mirror. I have to change myself, I repeated every night before going to sleep, crying for hours on end. The time has finally come to explain why.

I left my country for Canada, which I adopted as my homeland. I didn't really have any other choice because for eight years, I had no immigration documents allowing me to live as a free citizen. At the beginning of this hell, I hated the country that refused to grant me permanent residency from the depths of my heart. I wanted to leave and not come back until I wished to return, because of the cold and immeasurable heartbreak that led to all kinds of depression over the course of time. Today, I realized that God's plans are what they are, and if I had gotten these papers, I would be even more lost than when I landed here as just a fragile little bird without anyone I could count on. From an entire nation, the universe would choose me and allow me to leave my family and my daily life to open doors in a country completely different from my own through a man and his great love for me. Initially, he simply had hope and certainty that he would build a better future with me, even though he was aware that I didn't love him. He persisted, thinking that one day I would finally realize that I loved him and he was good for me. Yet I told him a million times that I didn't love him, but once again, you should know that God's plans are such that they must follow the course of history.

I had started my term in hotel administration at a college in the heart of downtown Montreal when I met a woman from Quebec, who showed me how to become a real Canadian bad girl by introducing me into the city's erotic massage parlours for one of the most profitable and extremely risqué massages. At the end the client expected a little more fun that transgressed all morality. I didn't stay there for long, just three months were enough for me to realize that I didn't really belong in that environment. It took only a summer to earn some money and imagine that I could succeed by myself without anyone's help. Not long afterward, I knew I had to make a choice because of my ex, who was still in the background.

That man, who had helped me enter and take care of many needs, which created a pressure that was starting to weigh on me, quickly left. I was sick and tired of always feeling the pressure my family was putting on me, and my new situation wasn't making our relationship any easier—it was growing more tense with each of our phone conversations. I joined him in Dominican Republic one last time, and I realized that he disgusted me more than anything else. I was only twenty and he, forty-five. What he wanted from me was simply beyond my strength. He was white. He had a lot of money. Despite his advanced age, he remained a very handsome man. He had sky blue eyes that would have melted the hearts of most of the women in my country; they would not have hesitated one second to give him as many babies as he wanted without complaining. The only problem came from me—I didn't love him. Sometimes I asked God in my prayers why he was not helping me accept my fate and marry this man without making a big deal about it. He loved me so intensely that he would have given his life just to see me smile. I had gotten used to luxury for two years before even going to Canada. I had all the cars I wanted thanks to his position in my original homeland. I lived in a big house and was surrounded by drivers and servants. I knew that with him I would never have to work in my life, but I refused to accept that decision. I was always unhappy when we were together. Without understanding why most of the time, I felt that my destiny lay elsewhere. During that time, I never thought that I would one day become one of the most famous writers in the world. I had no family to support me. Just before I left the country, my father died of old age, which made my future even more uncertain. God had become my only strength, but, at times, to be honest, I trusted the beauty he had given me more than him. I felt that I had inside me, despite some of my bad decisions, something I rarely saw in others but whose meaning always escaped me. Upon leaving the Dominican Republic, I announce the end of our relationship to my ex. I expected that he would cut me off, and I had prepared myself accordingly; I knew what the results of this decision would be. Indeed, he told me that I would now face my problems alone. I didn't complain; he wasn't my father, and he had already done some things that few men would do because ultimately, everything we do must benefit us in some way, shouldn't it? When he stopped sending me money every month, it automatically meant the end of my payments to my sister-in-law I was living with. The criticism wasn't long in coming. I couldn't explain to my family that I knew how to make money easily under-the-table without them discovering the truth. At the time, I knew that they never would have never approved of this direction, which was dangerous for my life and reputation. I found myself in the situation of having nobody to rely on but myself.

I spoke to no one of my new situation until my friend offer to share an apartment. I hastened to accept without thinking about the consequences. Once my decision was made, I told my family that I was leaving home. Three months after having started doing massages, my half-brother asked me never to set foot in his house again. I looked at him without blinking because I wanted him to know that I had become an adult and that things would no longer work as his wife wished. I picked up my belongings and, after a few months under his roof, I left for parts unknown.

My only influence was that one friend, who asked me to continue the massages in the apartment where we lived. We needed to be able to pay our bills and eat. I realized much later the major profit that I represented for the girl I considered my friend at the time. I was on very bad terms with my family. I was very young and very resentful. I resigned myself to continuing alone without speaking to anyone anymore. I didn't have many options because once she was free of all constraints, my very dear and devoted friend eagerly told me about her wonderful initiative of publishing the massages on the Internet, which I would have no choice but to perform. I can assure you that once the massages were performed in our apartment, the men who came demanded much more than a little handjob. Most of them wanted to leave having had a full-service massage, which at first, I refused. My friend, who wanted to have complete control over my profitability, began to suggest that I give more than what I was offering. I knew that I couldn't go back, and I wasn't ready to go back to my country. Reluctantly, I agreed to hear her out, and I then began to engage in prostitution, not knowing what to do and having no other place to go. Most of the time, I was left alone in the apartment because she went to her parents' house, and I always ended up falling asleep while crying my eyes out . . . I had gone from weighing 120 pounds to ninety pounds because I couldn't keep anything down. I prayed, asking God to forgive me for having behaved so stupidly, and I asked him to help me change the situation, which was swallowing me whole. After a week, one of the clients who came to see me for the same reasons was a very rich German. He owned one of the largest restaurants in one of the most exclusive neighborhoods on the south shore of Montreal. He was the one that the universe decided to send me. The first time he received my services, he wanted to see me again for a second time. I nodded in assent with no hope of him taking me more seriously. It was three days before he came back. I had fallen severely ill a day earlier because of my tonsils. I remember that I couldn't even get up to go to the hospital that morning. My whole body was suffering greatly when I heard knocking at my door.

I had completely forgotten that he was supposed to come by. When he saw me crying and panicked to see him before me, and afraid he might rape me, he apologized and kindly offered to take me to see a doctor. At first, I refused; I couldn't reimburse hospital bills, and I didn't want to owe him anything in return.

He didn't insist, but he stayed half an hour with me, which touched me a lot more than he would have imagined. He came back again to see me three days later, and this time, he clearly and concisely asked me to put an end to all my dangerous activities. I had asked God's help, and he had sent it to me through that man. He also had enough money to get me out of the big mess I had gotten myself into. Unfortunately, he had been married for many years. Believe it or not, I was very afraid of becoming a homewrecker for a couple who had already been together for a long time. We continued to see each other secretly, and I only understood two months later all the love he felt for me when he asked his wife for a divorce. I begged him to not jump to conclusions about his marriage so quickly, but he got it in his head that I already belonged to him because of what he could offer me. He also was 42 years old, had two small girls, an ex-wife, and excess weight that disgusted me, and he came from a country where I would never want to live. He understood my sadness only too well when he looked at me. Many changes had occurred in my life in a very short time and, before jumping into another more serious phase of our relationship, he suggested going to visit my mother for a week. Perhaps he imagined that I needed advice . . . I think he expected me to come back to him more willing so that he could ask me to marry him. He paid for my plane ticket just before the end of my study visa. Upon arrival in my country, I could in no way explain to my mother what I had just experienced. All I did was silently cry in her arms talking about the German. I didn't hide from her that I didn't love him either. She knew me well enough to know that I would leave him if my feelings didn't change before returning to Montreal. She advised me despite everything, as a mother who wanted the best for her daughter, to marry him and become a good wife.

How can I explain to you what I felt during the day before leaving my country? Because, without understanding why, my sixth sense whispered to me that as I would not return home very soon and that I wouldn't see my mother again for a very long time. All day, I was inconsolable without being able to grasp the meaning of my intuitions. I took the plane again as confused as I had arrived, and five days after my return, an earthquake happened that sent the country into a state that had never been seen before. Yet again, I had to resign myself to marrying a man I didn't love. When I analyzed the catastrophic situation I had left, and the broad media coverage, it was a big relief to me. As selfish as it sounds, I must confess that this great misfortune granted me a visa extension to stay in Canada while living independently. That lifted a huge weight from my shoulders because I came to understand how lucky I was to not be forced to return home if I refused to marry an individual who threatened me with all kinds of blackmail. After three months of pressure from him, I told him that I couldn't stay with him. With him, I felt as if I had been taken hostage; he even kept track the times we slept together in a small notebook, as if I had become his favourite diversion. I cried to see how my life was not what I was hoping for as a child. I asked him to forgive me for not being able to return his love. I heard him tell me that I would not find another man like him, that I would be nothing without his help. Discouraged by all my refusals, he dropped out of my life.

You are now probably wondering if I resumed my previous activities? My answer is no. I eventually took control over the situation. First, I confronted my friend who thought she was going to continue squeezing all the money I earned out of me. Without difficulty, I kicked her out of the apartment; after the German, I had a little more clarity about the whole thing. I had no choice but to find another way of easily making money, and I didn't have a ton of options. For some people, it boils down to doing the same thing, but for me, it was a thousand times better when I decided to become a cabaret dancer. A month after my start in that walk of life, I came across a young Vietnamese man who shared my life for a year and caused me a host of problems, although I must admit that they were not as bad as my previous ones. He was my first real boyfriend from an age standpoint . . .

I won't use anyone's name. For this reason, I will name each of them using their nationality, and they will surely recognize themselves but will not be too offended. For some of them, who have a big head because of their position and because I'm just their ex, I must tell you that it's with no hard feelings . . .

The Vietnamese man is someone I met at the very beginning in the several strip clubs I frequented in Montreal. I wasn't madly in love with him, but I wanted to deal with my issues while being with a good guy. I was ready to give us a chance, or at least that's what I was telling myself. I moved in with him a few months before the end of my lease. He showed me how to work to earn the most money possible in that line of work, except that he wasn't really doing his part to help improve the situation. Very often, I had to pay the bills when he had spent all his savings when he went out with his friends. He had an internet gambling addiction, and sex lasted less than five minutes every time. I had always wanted to have my breasts redone, and the only way I found to avoid blowing all my money on that idiot was to put it into something that he wouldn't at all be able to covet. He had made me lose a lot of money, and I was starting to question a relationship that was going nowhere since I doubted ever wanting to marry him. I didn't take long in putting all my savings into my breasts and showing him that the source of money that he imagined having no longer existed. At the end of our relationship, he was beginning to take lots of pills, such as speed, ecstasy and others that I refused to touch. We fought because I refused to go with him to after-parties, which consisted of taking drugs and dancing like zombies until nine or ten in the morning. I didn't know how to tell him that I wanted us to break up because at times, I just wanted to kill him with my own two hands. We had stopped sleeping together for the previous few weeks, and a week after my breasts surgery, I decided to go with my best friend at the time to a small get-together. I met a Bulgarian I liked a lot and who accompanied us home. Since I had had a lot to drink, once we arrived in front of my building, I asked him to escort me to the gym on the top floor. I will spare you the details of what happened between us, but after fifteen minutes, my Vietnamese man entered the room. I never panicked so much in my life! Of course, I was drunk, and I was not thinking about the consequences that such an act could have had. But, thank God, he did not try to fight with the Bulgarian. I waited for him to leave again to get up from the splendid position that I'm now not very proud of having been in.

I asked him to leave, and I went back to the apartment. That night, I was ready to leave, but he prevented me. I was all worked up, and I apologized profusely. I still hope that he can one day forgive me. The next day,

I told him that I didn't want to stay with him, but despite everything, he didn't want me to leave. I didn't want to hear it because our relationship didn't make sense to me anymore. I thought that he had something in store that would surprise me after such a betrayal, and after a week of weighing the pros and cons, I left and that was the end of that relationship.

I had taken another apartment right in the downtown area thanks to a contact from one of my good customers. I'd started working again even more than before because after having my breasts done, I was getting double what I usually did. Three months after my move, I met another guy who remained, until 2015, my first great love.

I had been working from the very beginning in a small club in an English-speaking neighbourhood in Montreal, but for reasons beyond my control, I got mixed up in a fight between a girl that I hated and the same friend whom I considered to be my best friend.

I decided to get involved; therefore, the owner asked my friend and me to not set foot there for at least three months. I had to find another place of work and fast; I ended up in another small club in a city called Laval. After two weeks, when I began worrying about the amounts of money that were no longer enough, he appeared. I went on stage for my performance, and like magic, he entered the room at that moment. I had never come across him before that night, but the moment my eyes met his, magic happened, and my heart melted for the stranger. I really threw myself into it because I wanted nothing more than his attention. From the beginning, I think he was impressed by my beauty and the flexibility I showed in dancing because I was doing highly dangerous movements that didn't leave him indifferent.

To top it off, my eyes didn't leave him for an instant. Everything played to my advantage, and when I left the stage and walked toward him, I already saw the effect I had on him. I then innocently asked him to come back with me in private. I had so impressed and aroused him that I didn't have to ask him twice.

Once we were one-on-one, he told me a little about his life. He owned four restaurants and had a very busy life. At the end, he asked me if I wanted some dinner or even do something ordinary with him. I assented rather indifferently, but inside, I felt my heart pounding. I already wanted him even before knowing he had plenty of money; being aware of what he owned had not helped. He left me one hundred dollars and said that he was tired and had to go back. I had to know why he came to such a place, and I was not too shy about asking him. He explained to me that he was there out of pure kindness: he had accompanied a friend who was very insistent that he come, and because it had been a long time since he had laid eyes on such a pretty girl, he had taken the chance to talk to me, hoping that I wouldn't refuse. After his explanation, I convinced myself to give it try at least once and see him again to find out what kind of person he was. He left me his number and departed. From that moment on, I began to think more and more about him. Nevertheless, I didn't try to rush anything because I understood the importance of the game of seduction. Given what kind of man he was, showing I was pursuing him would do nothing to advance my situation with him. So, initially, I was patient and showed him that I was as busy as he was while making it clear that I didn't lack interest in him. We exchanged text messages from time to time and told each other about our respective lives, laughing at the funny parts and trying to understand others that weren't so amusing.

I left to work outside Montreal, and he took a day off to come meet me there. It was at this time that I met my best friend to this day, Sandra Simas. It was the Tunisian woman who introduced me to her at that time because she was as shy as I was, and we never would have started a conversation if it had not happened that way.

A few years later, she became my personal designer when I opened my offices in Los Angeles. I still remember early in my career when I had nobody to turn to, and she offered me some help when I needed it the most. I would just like to thank her for being there until the end. For all these reasons, she has become like a family member. The Greek man knew most of my friends at the time, and the idea that I could continue seeing them was impossible with him. I lost touch with Sandra for a while because of the whole ordeal, but fate brought us back together once again, and it's at that point that we became inseparable.

I think back to the man I loved and who wanted, as much as I did, to take the time to get to know one another. He was Greek, and he had an ex-wife he still sent large alimony payments and a little six-year-old girl. I was only twenty-three years old, and I didn't realize the magnitude of the situation. All I knew was the way my heart beat for the man I was ready to move mountains for if he asked me. When things began to grow more serious between us, he wanted to know my intentions about my job, which was becoming increasingly embarrassing for both of us. I had a work permit that I had not yet used, and I was ready to try anything to live with him. I didn't think too much about it, but I first asked to meet his daughter. He was very pleased with my initiative, but unfortunately, this first meeting was a real disaster. Having become extremely nervous, I had never imagined such a traumatic encounter! I wanted to show the whole world that I loved him, but his daughter, always between us, demanded constant attention from her father. I knew that I needed, above all, to make myself loved and accepted by the little white girl. She became very protective and jealous whenever I dared to get too close to the man I loved. After that catastrophic day, he no longer wanted to see me, and my world fell apart in the span of one day.

I'd started praying, and I was asking God, every morning and every night, to give me one last chance at a normal life and to experience a real love story. I promised him that if he let me have that chance, I wouldn't let it go this time. I will return to the church's path, and I will be a real example. Two weeks after our disastrous outing, he decided to bring me to meet his family for a second time. When he told me about his decision, I regained confidence in life, and after another week, I noticed that everything was going so well that I didn't want to wait anymore. I asked to move in with him. He couldn't believe it. For him too, this was a big step to take. Since his separation, he had never really considered living with another person. He was not too keen about it, but I saw that he was seriously thinking about my proposal. A week later, he called me to tell me his decision. He told me that he wanted to give it a shot. I couldn't believe it. I loved him even more for all that he was going to change in my life. I felt that we had made the best decision. He helped me get rid of my latest apartment. He made space for me in his drawers and in his life, and we began a new life as a couple. I relentlessly looked for work for many weeks, and after three months, they hired me at Sears. It was my first real job! I stayed there for three months, and I left to join a new lingerie company that only hired women.

Like all couples, we fought, but our biggest point of contention was marriage. For the first time in my life, I wanted a man to marry me with all my heart. After his first marriage, he didn't want to make a mistake, and I completely understood. Only God knows how much energy I invested in our relationship just see him smile when he returned home after working long hours. He was a true tyrant about not changing his situation; at times, I hated him for being so hard on me, and I loved him just as much, since he was far and away the only man to always push back against me. It was a weird feeling that made me weep most of the time when he left me to return to work. I didn't know how to deal with all his refusals, and I became very unpleasant. I wanted to have his babies and never let him go, but at the same time, I didn't want to stay just be the girlfriend at his side when all his friends were married and were waiting for their next babies. I had broken off contact with all my friends, and most of the time, I had no one to confide in.

Of course, I had forgotten all the wonderful promises to God I had made, and I had not even once returned to thank him after getting what I wanted. Later, pray as I would, none of my wishes came true. I became extremely jealous for all kinds of reasons. I didn't see him often because his restaurants took up all his time, and what he gave me, I shared with his daughter, who lived in the house three days out of the week. I had wanted to be part of his life, and I often reproached myself for it. Now I loved a man who looked at me like a child most of the time and clearly made me understand during each of my tantrums that I could leave if our situation was no longer making me happy.

Is life unfair? I'm not ready to answer that question because you must also analyze all the disappointments you have lived through as much as I do and wonder where the fault lies. Why would I be the exception to the rule? We all have our own problems. Who is ultimately to blame?

Oh! I am not suggesting that he didn't help me progress. That is far from being the case. On the contrary, he allowed me to get out of the dancing scene for the short time that we were together. I am still grateful because it was only after him that I realized how well I could get by without being a slave of a money that was absolutely worthless. I managed to obtain my driver's licence thanks to his encouragement. I bought my first small car, which he also contributed to. Compared to my previous relationships, I never indulged in useless whims because I wanted to show him that I was expecting a lot more than simple gifts. I wanted to share my whole life with him and give him all the other children that would make me his real family and him, mine.

I'm not Cinderella, and he was not the prince that I imagined he would become for me. So, a year after moving in with him, I wanted to leave. I thought maybe it would help him understand that he was losing a good woman and that he would ask me to become his wife. Unfortunately, for certain people, good women can be found just about everywhere. I got along very well with some of his friends. His parents were not without feelings for me, and I believe that his daughter and I had become much closer. There were a few disasters, such as the only time I went with him to a wedding: I remember having had so much to drink that I sulked the whole time, reproaching him for not being a man because he refused to marry me. I lost my camera at the same time, and God only knows how many racy pictures were in it!

He abruptly left the wedding because of me, and of course, I can imagine that he was just about ready to kill me. I blamed myself for having acted like a child for years. There were only a few other times I got drunk at other weddings because of these past mistakes. The wedding was partly a lesson to me. At the end of our relationship, I went to Toronto with his parents and daughter; it was just another disaster. I didn't understand why I had to share him with so many people, because in my mind, it was our vacation. I drove him crazy with anger and wasn't at all embarrassed about sulking every day. I felt bad, and I wanted him to share exactly the same emotions I was feeling. I had never so desperately loved a man in my entire life. I couldn't believe that my heart could be so attached to a person like him. I didn't understand him, or at least, I didn't want to understand him. When we returned from Toronto, I told him that I was leaving him. He didn't even try to stop me, which broke my heart. I found a small apartment in his area in case he changed his mind, and I settled in. I had kept my job at La Vie en Rose, and since I couldn't pay for everything with the little that I earned, I started dancing again.

A few times, he stopped by to see me, but only because I begged him to come. But as the days went by, I was less and less able to get in touch with him. It was at this time that my regrets about having left began to weigh on my conscience.

Many times, my family blamed me for not knowing what I wanted. I now know, after a little investigating, that shortly afterward, he was dating his daughter's swim teacher. He had hired her a few months before our separation, which made me think that he had begun to see her when he was involved with me. One thing is for sure: cheaters will never change. He repeated his previous mistakes; that was the reason that he had gotten divorced from Georgia. I nevertheless grew quite depressed.

I can't explain why, but everything I'm still conscious of relates to a dream. A month after settling into that little apartment, I had the most incredible one. I saw myself in the White House, much older than I was at the time. I was talking with the first lady of the United States of America. It's amazing how we must pay attention to certain details that can't remain in the shadows—like the woman's blond hair, her advanced age and the kindness she emanated. They were specific images that I couldn't miss. I felt so important and blessed that I turned to look around me. Then I saw the cast of bodyguards in the room who were hurrying us to get the meeting going. I didn't understand why I had such a dream. Today, I know that my mind had travelled in time to help me understand why I had to continue on alone. All my active senses propelled me out of the dream. I had experienced what we call a premonition of the sixth dimension, and the feeling stayed with me for years.

I talked to my mother about it, and the only response I got from her was this simple sentence: "My daughter Mélissa, I've been watching you since your childhood, and I also know that nothing is impossible for God. If he allowed you to see this dream, he planned the timing for you to experience it fully."

I thought about it every day before really experiencing it now. I had also dreamed about the world war on two occasions. I was fleeing as I saw the world collapsing behind me. At the time, I'd wake up in a sweat and just ask God to spare us that calamity. Again, what must happen will happen, and no one can change it.

The last two little girls of my parents left my country to be adopted by one of my half-sisters who, for health reasons, couldn't bear children. Each of them left our home at the age of four to live in Canada. Being separated from those two little girls I had taken care of since their births greatly affected me. Unfortunately, I had no say in the matter—perhaps it was better that way. I remember that because of their departure I had started, around the age of seven, praying and asking for everything to fall into place so that one day I would be able to go and meet them to tell them the truth. My stepsister, when she adopted them, thought that we would never be able to enter Canada to see them again; she never admitted to them the truth about their origin. The saddest thing of all is that she even changed their first names and moved so far away that she imagined she was beyond any danger from us. I think that God listened to the prayers of a poor little broken-hearted girl crying in her bed when no one was there to hear her tears in the dark. I've never really had a lot of friends because I very often aroused jealousy in other girls. For years, I had grown used to confiding in this lone supernatural power that I felt acting all around me, but whom I couldn't in any way see. I told him about everything, but the day that I started to believe that God really existed was when I left my country. Since I was seven, I begged him in my prayers to allow me to one day go to the same country as my two little sisters. I wanted to see them again because, as the years passed, I felt that they had become strangers—but my heart refused to give up. I wanted to share my childhood with my little sisters and learn to laugh, cry and fight with them. But above all, I wanted to bond with them and figure out how to become friends even after all that time.

In 2018, I knew exactly the reason why I was on Earth. My brother Jhonny could not have enjoyed as full a life if I hadn't been so involved. I had promised him that I would never abandon him. I kept my promise to the end without ever being disheartened. He had always suffered from mental disability, but by studying him, I had already seen his talent. As soon as he immigrated to America, I kept encouraging him to make a career out of wrestling. He surprised even himself by winning two trophies and becoming world champion toward the end of his career. He married an Italian, and they had three beautiful children. My big brother changed and became a father and great husband I was very proud of.

Are you wondering why in this case I didn't resolve to follow God after entering the country in question? I was not yet ready to do so, and if I had, I wouldn't have any story to tell you today. His goal was to have an impact on the world and change lives with the story of a simple girl from the South.

To follow up on my dream about the White House, a week later, the older of my adopted little sisters, Lindsay, contacted me herself and told me about the news that she had learned the day before she decided to get in touch with me. Thank God, at that time, I already had a car. After her call, I couldn't sleep because all I wanted was to see her. Nineteen years had passed, and my prayers had finally been answered. I realized that I would finally be able to hold her in my arms and tell her how much I had been praying for that day. I got dressed, and I went to pick her up to go downtown.

We talked about the years that had passed for the entire night without ever wanting to stop. Given her young age, I was happy to know that she wasn't taking drugs or suffering from any sort of addiction. She explained that she had endured a host of injustices during her childhood, but she had learned good lessons from them. I wasn't ready to have my stepsister on my back, so I asked my sister to keep our meeting secret.

I sometimes accompanied Sosie, my assistant manager, a wonderful old woman of Armenian descent who had a role in hiring me at La Vie En Rose and who loved me with all her heart, in a small prayer circle. I could hardly make any progress in my life because I just couldn't forget the Greek.

I was praying for a miracle that never happened. Nevertheless, I spoke to Lindsay about it and asked her to accompany me so that we could pray together. It was at that point that she spoke to me about the PQL Action Centre (Liberating Word Ministry). I was very reluctant about this new church, so much so that the day I went to pick her up, I remember complaining about it for the duration of the trip; I was looking for any little sign to just turn around. I have often wondered why God allowed me to wait for my little sister to come back to act so radically on my life.

I have concluded that I wouldn't have followed anyone because, quite simply, I only had acquaintances, and the only friend I had associated with during all my years in Canada had become addicted to cocaine. I had tried some drugs, such as ecstasy, speed, cocaine—but by far my favourite was a little joint from time to time. I was the older sister of three girls who were counting on me as a role model. I couldn't give up because of them, and I didn't give myself the right to do so. Upon entering the centre for the first time with my sister, I didn't understand what I was called on to become. The building was like no other religious place I had been to before then.

It didn't have a cross on the outside, and I won't forget to mention how I discovered a completely modern church for the first time. I want you to know that at that time, I wasn't at all happy with my life, but one thing was certain: I knew how to earn money, and I had enough to meet my needs. I was not living healthily, but I was very logical. I wasn't doing well in some ways, but when I thought about those who were much worse off, I plucked up my courage. I continued to live in a world where I was slowly losing myself just to be able to pay the bills and continually buy unnecessary things. I had a good salary, given that I left with at least five to six hundred dollars on a bad night and seven to nine hundred on the best nights. Despite this situation, it did not prevent me from continuing to believe in God. I sometimes doubted him, but I thought he must love me deeply and more than most if he had created me so different, beautiful and intelligent. I didn't ask him for too much aside from watching over me and my family. My only goal was to gather enough money to bring over my mother, my little sister Jenny and big brother Jhonny, who were still living there and whose lives were not a bed of roses. I had my share of problems, but I could eat, clothe myself and sleep without thinking about the next day. Until that morning, I had never experienced such a special face-to-face encounter with the Creator. During the service, I knew exactly what he wanted from me. The only problem was that it couldn't have been crazier to follow. I returned almost every Sunday because I constantly had unanswered questions in my head. My expectations were growing and became much greater for He who wanted me to become a servant and an example for others.

You must understand that my situation had not changed. Every year, I received a work permit that had to be renewed before the expiry date. Following a lawyer's advice, I sent an application for residence on humanitarian grounds, and one day before Christmas 2012, an immigration officer phoned to tell me that my request had been denied. I should expect to be deported back home at any time. I had to endure the most awful Christmas that year, but despite all that, I didn't lose faith. The more I returned to church, the dirtier I felt to be sitting among Christians and acting like I was one of the saints. I called my step-brother from the very beginning of the story, who had eventually begun talking to me again, and I asked him to let me come back to live with them. They agreed, and I moved a few weeks later, telling myself that I had to walk in the ways of the Lord. I settled in with them yet again while making good resolutions for a new start. For the New Year's, my best friend asked me to accompany her to a party downtown. I didn't really want to take part, but I thought the time was right to make her understand that our friendship could no longer continue. I went to the club with only one intention: emptying my heart and telling her that we wouldn't be friends anymore from then on; her life was steamrolling mine. When I arrived at the door of the club, I came across the Italian man who would become my last serious relationship in Montreal.

When I saw him, my heart skipped a beat, much like the first night with the Greek. At that moment, I smiled inwardly and told myself that in the end, everything was perhaps not lost! When he opened the door, I noticed that my friend was behind him. I was automatically shocked because I wasn't intending to go anywhere with a guy who was already interested in one of my friends. With regret, I entered the club. I got very drunk that night while trying to forget the only man who had become inaccessible in my eyes. I had stopped smoking, but because I was quite drunk, I accompanied my friend, and I gave myself permission to have a cigarette. We had a short conversation during which I listened to her boasting about going out with the Italian and having manipulated and never loved him. She called him a "fag" during the entire conversation, and she confessed that after the party, she was going to sleep at his house because she didn't really know where else to sleep. I started thinking about life's unfairness, and it made me sick. I couldn't tell her that I had just experienced love at first sight with the same guy without the risk of angering her.

When the party was over, I ended up accepting the proposal of going to bed with a young Jew that I liked, but I knew that our night would lead to nothing. When I woke up the next day at the W Hotel, I got a call from my friend inviting me to go to breakfast with her and the Italian. I hastened to accept the invitation because I was thinking that I just had to see him one last time. The three of us were sitting together, and I kept telling myself that he was just one among many insignificant men, but I knew I was lying to myself and that, above all, I was winning over my friend's ex. I was nevertheless resigned to letting it go and moving on to the next step, which was getting back to God. I was no longer as enthusiastic about my new resolution that I had taken two days before getting to know this new guy, but because my friend had become the obstacle, I thought that it was perhaps better that way. I went home to my brother's house repeating to myself that I was taking the right path. I realized two weeks later that the Italian had also succumbed to my charms. Curious to know who I was and where I was from, he asked my friend about me and only got answers, such as, "You don't know that girl. She's a slut. She sleeps with everyone, and the worst is that she rejects them once she finds better prey."

Are you wondering how I learned all this? Well, would you believe that my friend had miscalculated her move? Let me explain the situation from the beginning. She only became aware of her mistake of letting some major advantages slip away with that guy after coming across him that night. She had preferred to let him go because he did not sufficiently meet her criteria. He had just bought a house, and she could not bear sleeping on the floor with him, but he soon acquired everything a woman looks for in this superficial world. When I met him, he already lived in a big house with a jacuzzi, a Porsche parked in the garage, an Escalade, an X5, the other big pickup, the years' hot motorcycle, and above all, a boat. Returning home after that party, she confided her regrets to me about having acted selfishly and left him because of poor judgment. When the Italian showed her his fondness for me, once again, she wanted to use me for her own ends: She asked me, when he did not return her calls, to contact him for her. I did so wholeheartedly and without a second thought at first because I had resigned myself to not playing a nasty trick on that girl. But I was in for a big shock when I discovered the words my friend used to describe me when he began asking me very personal questions while admitting to me that he already had the answers. It was at that point that I joyfully gave myself over to embracing the one person that had recently made my heart flutter. I went to his home one evening on his invitation, and I slept in his bed. I will avoid sharing unnecessary details, knowing that your minds will be able to do so on their own. After such an embarrassing act, I felt so dirty that I cried my eyes out for at least an hour in my car in front of my step-brother's house. I was questioning the kind of person I had become. I pulled out my cell phone, and I wrote the truth to my friend, not because I wanted to continue talking to her but to forget what I had just done; I was not her. I asked her to forgive me, which she, of course, refused to do, and I understood that I was doing her as much harm as she had done to me by bad-mouthing me behind my back. It wasn't the first time she had done something like that to me. I was sure that I didn't want this girl in my circle of friends. On each of the different occasions that made me push her away by clearly explaining that we would stop being friends, she would always turn a deaf ear and find her way back to me. That girl embodied everything that was bad in my eyes: alcohol, drugs, sex, dancing and how she would never let an opportunity pass of finding a way to take advantage of a situation. None of my exes ever liked her, and I was always asked to choose: her or the relationship. This situation with the Italian had become the only way to help me get rid of this Tunisian woman. It was what could be called a blessing in disguise, and I was quite thrilled. I admit that during the first year of the separation, I nevertheless missed that unhealthy friendship because she had always been my only confidant. I couldn't tell my little sister everything that I had done in my past, but with her, I didn't even need to say much for us to understand each other because we had been in the same boat from the very beginning. Except that I had arrived at a point where I had to leave the boat to escape a shipwreck caused by wanting to cling to everything that was not part of my values.

You are thinking that I went out with the Italian once this girl was no longer in the picture—my answer is still no, or more accurately not right away.

I lost sight of him for almost a year because after telling my friend the truth, the situation turned into a living hell for him and me. Starting by begging him to take her back with all kinds of threats, she harassed him for all sorts of reasons. She called him all a bunch of names for having gotten involved and having ruined our long-standing relationship. He was so overwhelmed that he didn't want to have any contact with either one of us.

I accepted his decision as a sign of fate, and for almost a year, I completely stopped dancing; I focused on living a normal life while attending church. I no longer shared any man's bed, and I no longer wanted to leave my brother's home. My family thought that I had gone completely crazy, but personally, for some inexplicable reason, I believed from the bottom of my heart in a true change. I had questions that always remained unanswered because I didn't know how to answer them myself. Like, for example, knowing my purpose in life.

I didn't know what I wanted to be, and my biggest fear was to die without accomplishing anything on this Earth. I no longer wanted to continue being a disgrace to God and my mother, who was counting too much on my potential.

Nine months after I had joined the Action Centre, I received the long-awaited answer. For this, I did crazy things, such as donating all my jewels, gold, diamonds and money, and I haven't regretted it even once. Just after my gifts, stories of all kinds began to occupy my mind, but it was too much effort to write them down. I wrote one of them when, oddly enough, my brother's computer died.

I had lost my story, and the first fruit of my work was gone. Today, I know that God did not want this first story to come out before The Legend of the Soul Sisters. I didn't understand at the time because I was not surrounded by people of faith to help me in my new spiritual journey and to avoid giving up, except for my mother who, alas, was too far away and unable to assist me in any matter. After nine months without a work permit renewal and without money coming in, I began to feel the problems. It started with my car, which broke down. Do I even need to mention being pursued by my phone company for a large sum of money for my recent unpaid bills? The little money I had saved evaporated because I wanted to repay my sister-in-law's hospitality. Not once did she imagine that this money could have been used to deal with my many problems. I had moved to their home bringing the few things that I still cared about, such as some paintings, my large TV, my clothes and other appliances that I was still saving for a future move.

I don't like taking advantage of the kindness of others—I don't like feeling dependent on others either. I didn't have much to offer her in exchange for room and board. The only means I had to do so was to leave her the few things that I still owned.

I offered for her to keep them after many calculations, thinking that it was for the best, without her sensing what she was doing to me. She accepted them without embarrassment. I was suffering inside, but given what I was going through, it was impossible not to offer them to her. This period of my life was the worst because, being with the Lord, I was asked not to judge. In any case, I could no longer have doubts about these various facts, which seemed quite crazy in some respects, but analyzing them now, I can just give thanks to God for allowing me to go down this path unharmed. I am also grateful to Him for allowing my big brother Jimmy to enter Canada because of the disasters that happened in our country. Without him, who knows what would have become of me? He was in the same situation as I was with immigration, which did not prevent us from helping each other when we could. We were a family, and blood ties are what they are. I moved into his house for a while but left because of his life with his wife and their children. Seeing my life turning into a disaster, I didn't know what to do anymore because I was following a god who wasn't making his presence felt.

I had lost everything that was dear to me from one day to the next. My family didn't understand me anymore because I was trying above all to convince everyone without much success to put themselves in my shoes. I had ended up frightening my little sister, who wouldn't talk to me anymore. I was completely broke. I owed my brother money because he had helped me solve my car problem. I had started to write little stories that I gave up on after a few pages because of a lack of interest in finishing them.

In small fragments, I began The Legend of the Soul Sisters and My Precious during the summer of 2013. I didn't yet know what they would become because most of the time, I was so lacking in inspiration, and I didn't yet understand the greatness of the two stories.

My world collapsed for almost a year. I was wondering where God had gone. My doubts on the pros and cons of my choices began again shortly after. I absolutely had to regain control; I couldn't trust a being that I wasn't even able to see.

I left my brother Jimmy's residence to return once again to my first sister-in-law's home. Soon after, she also moved to a small area called Mascouche, which was far from all I knew and even the PQL Action Centre. She eagerly asked me to come back because she needed my help with the children. She began by asking me to go pick one of them up at school or to bring the other to daycare. The times when I was a little reluctant and answered that I wasn't sure I would be able to, I suddenly felt a tension building between us. After ten months of my journey at the Action Centre, I dispiritedly went back down the path of clubs with nude dancers. Nevertheless, I asked God to forgive my mistakes.

I had nobody to turn to and didn't have any other ways of getting out of my situation. I no longer returned to the Centre because I couldn't fake it. I contacted my little sister and told her that I was moving in with her. Three months before my call, she had found a small three-room apartment in Saint-Leonard in Montreal that she could barely pay for. She eagerly asked me to move in with her because we understood each other without speaking.

We had been able to deal with our various, occasional squabbles by trying to resolve them as best we could. I had my principles, and she was still very young. She had just turned twenty and I, twenty-five. She had always had everything without having to worry about anything, and I always had needed to fight for everything. I was back, because of my life circumstances, in an environment that horrified me, and I wept every night since I had returned. I had started working again in the same small club in an English-speaking area of Montreal when I came across the Italian, who didn't live far from there. I was glad to meet him because I hadn't slept with anyone up to that day. I knew that the feelings I had for him were still present since I unsuccessfully pursued him again for two more months. Christmas was approaching fast. I felt sad to not be with someone and always chasing after the wrong people. The first week I came to Canada, I met a young Quebecer, who had since joined the Canadian Army. He resumed contact with me that Christmas, and his presence helped me forget the Italian's existence. The only problem was that he had been married for a year and was only going through a rough patch with his wife.

I didn't go out with him in the beginning because I preferred the Greek, and for this reason, he had never forgiven me. He told me that he had resigned himself to marrying that girl after being rejected.

I regretted not having picked him because I thought that at this time, he would have married me and not another woman. I had agreed to see him again because he swore to me that it was truly over between them. I decided to invite him to spend Christmas with my family, and he reciprocated, inviting me to meet his parents for New Year's.

I started to regain my appetite for life after so many months of pain and misery; the only downside was waiting for his divorce so that he could marry me. The soldier lived eight hours from Montreal in a small, even more remote area north of Toronto called Barry. When after New Year's he returned home, I was thinking about nothing but going to meet up with him. I had to earn some money at all costs because I'd just started dancing again. He wasn't stupid and quickly realized that I was never home at night. He started by reproaching me for the night life that was beneath his values. I understood him perfectly, and I offered to come to see him to see if it would work out between us.

I took a train and a bus on a whim, and off I went. I was glowing with happiness when I saw him. It was wrong of me, but I didn't feel bad for a second about his wife, and I wanted him to get rid of her quickly, so I could take her place. The reason for the conflict was that she had become a Baptist and wanted him to return to the Church just like her. I knew one day I would return to God, but for the moment, I needed to find a husband. Except that God has different plans for each of us, and I strongly believe that the Quebecer's wife loved him just as much as I did and maybe even more than I showed him. Compared to me, despite all her problems, she never broke her promise to continue serving God. The Italian called me to check up on me, but I felt great joy to announce my departure from Montreal and my love for someone else who was much more worthwhile than he was. When he realized that he was no longer part of my world, he quickly asked me to come back to talk about our disagreement. After a month of life in Barry, I was questioning the kind of life that I really wished to live. I shared the life of a married man, and I noticed, above all, how my situation was becoming even more serious than before. I wasn't working, and I was wondering what I was going to do there. Going back to dancing wasn't even possible with him, and I absolutely had to know where our two life journeys were taking us. He could never make a decision about the relationship with his wife. My little sister's birthday was just around the corner, so I didn't question it: I told him that I was going home. He asked me if I was sure I was making the right decision. I replied that I wasn't but that I would also leave him some time to think about our situation. I took the train, and I went home. The day after my return, he called me to tell me that he was getting back together with his wife. I was sad, very sad, but not surprised because I knew that God was teaching me yet another life lesson. When he learned that I was back in Montreal, the Italian said that he couldn't let me leave again, and he began calling me incessantly. I had just simply stopped loving him. I was mad at the whole world that I had yet again behaved like a real idiot. I was angry with him for not having gone out with me before the Quebecois contacted me around Christmas time. He became so insistent that a month later I figured I might as well give it a go, and I became his girlfriend.

We got to know each other better. Sometimes, we laughed together, but I mainly wept in his arms when things weren't going well. He eventually became very affectionate. I didn't understand why he wouldn't give us a chance to move forward together by marrying me. He had no desire to help me get out of my situation, even if he knew the time I had waited for him to finally decide to take me seriously. It's too bad because he will never understand what kind of person I could have become for him. He told me that he was jealous that I was dancing but did nothing to change the situation. Knowing how I took care of his home when he was away, he soon asked me to move in with him. He imagined that I must be one among many who wanted to live in a big house on the west side of the island. I was ready to settle down but only if he married me. I had run out of patience with men like him because I was starting to understand their true nature. I didn't want to make the same mistakes anymore. I had suffered enough from all the pieces that had never really been put back together. The more I realized that my relationship with him was going nowhere, the more I pressured him so that he would get out of my life. He introduced me to his parents, and one thing was certain: his father's obvious racism toward my origins. He made very shocking comments the first time that I talked to him, for example, "I don't have enough room to feed your whole family. You shouldn't bring all of them to my home." He made some other comments that aren't worth the effort of writing about. I still wanted to have a child with the Italian, and I got the following answer from him: "You have no career. You're just a dancer. I have everything."

For a few months, I tried to convince myself that maybe he had some feelings for me. Otherwise, why was he still there in my life, or even, why did he make the effort of introducing me to his parents? Because I couldn't find answers to these questions, I eventually made him understand very clearly that he had to decide. Our game had to go to the next level or end it and allow both of us to move on and go our own ways. He had to decide to either marry me and help me stop dancing so that I could seriously get to work on my book, which was clearing taking shape in my mind or let me go and get used to it since he alone could change the situation. He replied affirmatively.

I was delighted that he decided for once to make the right choice. We set a date to go buy the rings, and he resigned himself to coming with me. Once we were in front of the jewelry store, he changed his mind. The situation was hopeless because he thought that I was after him for his money. That afternoon, I cried my eyes out on St-Hubert Street all the way back to the car. That was the end of our short romance.

Someone already told me of a ritual held every year by the owners of the small English-speaking club where I was still working that ensured they never lost their customers. I don't know why this information made its way to my ears; it was if I had to know that the place did not work like all the other clubs in Montreal. I had noticed, whenever I was forced to leave that place because they prevented me from coming back there for at least three months, something positive would always happen to me. The small club was one of the places that brought in more people than anywhere else. Inside most of the people there, I saw unfortunate souls who returned again and again for years without ever understanding why. Even though I was not the best person to tell them about God, I did it anyway. Some of them were hooked on cocaine or women, and I strove to make them aware that they were going down the wrong path. I continued to dance for three months after my breakup with the Italian. The owner fired me from the club at the end of the second month, just before Christmas. I had a lot of things to pay for, so I didn't take long to start up with another small club on the South Shore of Montreal. I found myself in another club making much more money than most of the girls, but I was increasingly unhappy to have to continue in that line of work. I was deeply troubled to see how most of the women had a serious cocaine addiction. I had rarely seen people who were so open about repeatedly taking drugs without worrying about the impact it had on their families when they were at home. Ninety-five percent of them were mothers, sisters, and daughters and had to set some kind of example in their homes. I couldn't ask them to stop using because they would never have listened to me and on top of it, I would have made a lot of enemies.

I understood that God had chosen me to become the light. As soon as I set foot in the club, I was always beside myself. I knew I had to stop coming back there. I kept telling myself that it was now or never because I needed to become an example for all those women who were very often beaten by men who were taking advantage of them—pathetic guys who were abusing them, using all their money without understanding that they were selling their bodies and souls to try to hold on to them. They were women who did not know why they were selling the temple of God. Most of them were no longer ashamed to show themselves naked. They were lost and were so far from the light that they could no longer see it shine. Not long afterward, I returned to the ways of the church. I had completely stopped dancing before Christmas, and I focused on my passion for writing, promising God that I wouldn't give myself to any other man until the day when he decided that my path would cross the only person who would be inaccessible to me. You can probably guess right now who it could have been based on what I've told you about him if things hadn't been so complicated in my life.

Now let me enlighten you on some things you might not yet know about me. In November 2014, I had lost my work permit and was expecting to be asked to leave at any time to return to a country that was becoming increasingly dangerous. When I got sick, I couldn't consider going to a doctor unless I could pay him under the table. I had lived in Canada for eight years, and I was integrated into the culture as if it had always been part of my life.

I had a dream that was my only hope, and my trust was in a God who many of you would have simply refused to give a chance. All these years, I had kept one friend among all the men I knew because I saw the good in him, and I want to mention his name because he has remained one of my best friends to this day. François Rainville had become for me someone I desperately wanted to develop feelings of love for, but my heart flatly refused to go along with my reason.

I knew that he had been madly in love with me at one time, and when he saw me in the phase of deportation, he wanted to help me by proposing marriage. Long before my best friend's proposal, I could have, with all the money I earned in bars at that time, ended up marrying someone by paying them. However, I always rejected that option because, for me, marriage was one of the most sacred things and is even more so now in my eyes. I wanted to marry someone who would make my heart thrill; I had always sworn to myself that once we were married, I would never let him go. The option to marrying my best friend was inconceivable despite all the advice given to me because of the things that could have changed for the worse at any moment if I were deported from Canada. Even with all these problems, I kept my faith in He who allowed me to come here for the sole purpose of becoming the most influential undocumented immigrant author in the contemporary literary world.

Before the end of that same year, I had met a Persian and any girl would have given up everything to join him in Vancouver. According to the plans, and because of our endless daily telephone conversations that were extremely thought provoking, I would move in with him if things continued to work well between us for long enough. I knew with certainty that it was still my choice and not God's, when a month later, I got over him and, since that day, I've not stopped praying for one minute to be able to push aside all the enemy's other plans to make me fail to fulfill my true potential. My time became precious. Two weeks before the end of 2014, I started writing in the morning when I woke up, and I only stopped when my hands and bones made me give them some rest. From

December 31st, 2014, to January 1st, 2015, instead of being in a club, where most beautiful young women my age usually get together to party and drink, I spent my evenings at the PQL Action Center, very proud to be accountable to such a great universe. I can assure you that I was never so inspired as I was at the end of that year. I finished my first two books two months later, and I prayed day and night about the hundreds of pages I had written and that I was preparing to publish around the world two and a half years later. I questioned myself more than once about what I was going to reveal about my life and about how the world would perceive me after this book. I already knew the answer because I knew God wanted me to do it. I had to help other people that I knew throughout the world change their lives as God had changed mine. Not only women but also men who are married and who do not feel at all troubled about paying for the services of young women like me. There are men throughout the world who spend fortunes on their animal needs. There are many times in my life when I found myself offered large sums of money for all kinds of services that I immediately refused. Yet, a few times, I convinced myself to accept because I thought that the sums offered were worth it, but once I was in the hotel room with those men, nothing happened. Each time, I fervently offered up heartfelt prayers, begging God to forgive me and get me out of those hotel rooms without being the victim of any abuse. The mysterious ways of the world made it such that every time, the men in question couldn't even get an erection. I held on to these three different cases as examples. I can assure you that God is alive. He listens to prayers and acts in favour of all those who ask with faith. Often, when I start to pray, I raise my hands to heaven, and I profess my love for Him with these words, "I have not forgotten, Lord, and I give infinite thanks to your goodness for your divine protection that made this a day of joy, peace, praise, and not of misfortune for each of your children."

I would like to tell you that after having written my book, they sold, and I became a famous writer, but alas, after sending my books all over Quebec, they were turned down over nine times. I was still very naïve and needed to find out why, since I knew the high quality of my manuscripts. I finally convinced myself to talk about it with my sister-in-law's mother, who advised me to get it corrected by a professional. She put me in contact with Robert Morin, who has been my savior and angel. Of course, I had to pay for his help, but it allowed me to see things more clearly. I needed to put illustrations in The Legend of the Soul Sisters, but all these steps required money, and I didn't have any. What do you think was the first thought that came to mind? Yes, four months after all my resolutions, I started dancing again in a small club on the west side of the island. I was saving as much as I could and trying not to slip into depression most of the time. In September of that year, I met my second great love, Sylvano. He was just out of prison, and the same day, he came to the club with his friends. Indeed, despite my particular life journey, I had never been with a criminal in my life. He was tall, handsome, muscular, young and white, and quite intelligent for his twenty-nine years, and I was stupid enough to believe that he had changed. He very easily tilted any situation in his favour. I stuck with him for two and a half years, thinking it would develop into something more serious in my life. I left the club on the west side of the island to work in the biggest bar in downtown Montreal. It was the busiest club in Montreal, and I can tell you that at first, it was not easy to have a place there, but I succeeded thanks to one of the bosses who took me under his wing. Sylvano was hiding his double life and always made my life difficult. Thank God, I had to dig deeper to understand what kind of person I had been associating with for some time at that point. I was madly in love with him, but he had more than one relationship with various young women at the same time. I refused to accept this new insight into him just because I loved him. The more my feelings grew, the more the situation between us spun out of control. In the meantime, I prayed to be able to find someone who would want to illustrate my book. I was discouraged because the months went by fast, and my search was futile. Finally, one fine winter day, my car broke down. Reluctantly, I took the subway to get to the club when Patrice came and sat next to me to talk to me. I sang the praises of my fantasy novel and talked to him about my wish to include drawings in it. He asked me to contact him because he thought he had the right person for me. The next day, I got in touch with him, and three weeks later, he unearthed a fantastic artist for me.

Having been continually manipulated and ridiculed by Sylvano, I ended up meeting a Mexican at the club who lived in Vancouver. I had always wanted to visit that city, which I knew was one of the most interesting in Canada. Two months before meeting him, I gradually convinced myself to move to start something new again. Of all the others, the idea of going to Vancouver held the strongest appeal. So, when I ran into him, I took the opportunity to spend a little more time with him and succeed in convincing him to invite me to visit him in his town. He was by far the most handsome man I had ever dated in my life—he was also the craziest. Having become a long-time addict to the strongest drugs found in North America, his mood quite often radically shifted, but he never pressured me to take any. I had been taking hairdressing courses for several months to get out of my situation.

I had stopped seeing Silvano because of all his poor conduct, which had partly opened my eyes. A prime example was the weekend I went with him to Toronto to see The Weekend sing. After the concert, he left me to have sex with another girl who was in the box with our group. The next morning, when I realized this, I fought with his best friend, who always stuck up for him, and I left with his truck, leaving Silvano to return by train to Montreal. This is just one example of all the drama that took place between us! I desperately wanted to turn the page and towards the end of April, when the Mexican asked me to come visit him, I jumped at the invitation.

I went and stayed with him for two weeks. From then on, I knew that I absolutely had to give it a try. For myself, for my dreams, for the little flame in me that was not yet dead. What did I have to do for my documents? Nothing seemed to be happening in that area. I therefore contacted a new immigration officer, and to top it all off, I had to go before a judge to plead my case. A month later, I received protection from Canada without receiving my permanent residence card, but it was a small victory, which let me know that all was not lost. Six months later, the Mexican and I broke up. I must confess that, when I arrived in Vancouver, his mother, who lived in the same building as he did, categorically refused to meet me.

She called me a negress and all other sorts of names. She never wanted to give me a chance. I thought it was sad—but that's destiny. She wanted her son to get back together with his ex-girl friend whose family had an immense fortune in Vancouver.

I loved the Mexican but not as much as Sylvano, so I got used to the idea that it wasn't such a big loss after all. I couldn't help but think about Sylvano because everything in me was longing for him. Why does love makes us vulnerable to the point that truth matters little to us? I ended up going back to see him and trying to convince him to give us a chance. On his side, it was clear that a relationship with me wasn't going bring anything better to his life. He knew that I had given up my apartment over a month ago and that at any time I could leave Montreal. I was hoping with all my heart that he would keep me with him and that he would never let me leave. The future is unpredictable: we don't know why some things work out and others don't. After several unsuccessful attempts, I bought my ticket, and on December 12th, 2016, I landed in Vancouver with no one I could count on. I had become unattached, and at the same time, I had a heightened awareness of what I could accomplish if I focused on making the right choices. I stayed in a small hotel downtown while I looked for an apartment in the same area.

I visited a few, and finally, after four long days, I found the perfect apartment. It was right downtown in a rather upscale neighbourhood. To be honest, I was the problem: when I want something, nothing and no one can make me change my mind. Luckily, I had been able to save enough to allow myself to live in such a place! The book The Secret by Rhonda Byrne had recently really opened my eyes, and I was about to put some of her advice into practice. Even before arriving in Vancouver, I remember having drawn up a short list based on what I learned in the book of my goals for the coming months or even for the years to come. My list stated that by 2017, I would sign a deal for my first two books with a publisher in France, I would make my first million and even more. I had taken the decision to stop dancing, and I was hoping, from the depths of my heart, to no longer have to do it. For this reason, I had written on the list that I wanted to work as a waitress in one of the largest nightclubs in the city. That way, I would make a little money while calmly awaiting the answer from France. I had ended up spending a lot of money furnishing my new apartment, buying food and maintaining my lifestyle without going overboard. A month had passed, and I worked in one of the largest nightclubs in the city. Every day, I went back to a Starbucks to update The Legend. The book was a huge challenge for me because of my lack of knowledge about how to successfully incorporate the illustrations into the story. Being far away from everything and alone began to weigh on me, but I wasn't discouraged. I eventually contacted Bernard Gobin, someone I found on the internet who initially did not want to see me, but because of my pleas, he changed his mind and gave me a brief appointment the following week. I expected just about anything other than a Frenchman helping me in this town. Thank God, it made the explanations he gave me to help me succeed in my research easier to understand. For two hours, he taught me how to work with Word and Acrobat to complete my work. Before leaving, I told him that he would see me again and I would never forget what he had done for me. I promised him a job someday. He smiled at me and wished me good luck, as if to say it was a pipe dream.

I wasn't dreaming—I knew it. This was different. I followed his advice, and when I finished the work on February 2nd, 2017, I sent my book to more than six publishing houses in Paris. Fifteen days later, on February 17th, 2017, my book was accepted. The Vérone publishing house wanted my book, and two months later, the Percée publishing house also wrote asking me to sign with them. The miracle was happening. I was walking on air. Things were not always going as well as I wanted at the club, but at least this motivated me to be patient. I didn't think that I would ever see Sylvano again, but he called me to tell he had arrived in Vancouver on February 19. I was starting to forget him but not enough to be able to refuse to see him. I hadn't slept with anyone, and I terribly missed physical contact with him. He wanted to stay at my home. Without thinking, I accepted. I wanted him to be proud of me and want to someday introduce me to his parents.

The heart has its own reasons that reason does not know. As far back as I can remember, that sentence always seemed quite mysterious to me. Maybe one day I will understand it, but it always came to mind whenever I thought about Sylvano. The week with him was extraordinary. Everything seemed to be happening as if in a dream.

I remained very skeptical of his sudden interest in me. Two weeks after his departure, I lost my job at the club. The boss thought I was too shy, and I guess he wasn't too happy that I turned down big customers who always asked me to go home with them after my working hours. You are never very safe in my experience . . . I continued to be involved with Sylvano a month later. We fought on the phone like we did in the beginning: nothing had really changed. I felt stupid for having given him the keys to my apartment despite the comments of most of my best friends. I loved him much more than I thought. I didn't see him for months. I had a very clear idea of what I didn't want to go through anymore, and this was one of those experiences. I left my contact information all over the place to find work. I was in a new city whose rules were different than the ones in Montreal. I would like to write with pride that I had a bunch of offers, and that I didn't go back to doing the same things as before, but after three long months without a response in my job search, I returned to one of the biggest clubs in downtown Vancouver. All my friends from Montreal didn't really help me and advised me to go back to dancing. I had nobody to turn to, and moreover, I never really have had anyone. My only consolation was that one day my books would make their way in the world, and I would live freely. I realized that with my strong temperament, I couldn't have a boss.

Life isn't the same for everyone, and you shouldn't wait for a miracle because one day it may be too late. Instead, you need to make it happen by thinking that you were born for it. That has always been my central theory. Nevertheless, I continued with this book because I needed to publish it that same year. Mr. Morin had already corrected it, but I had to make further modifications. I didn't waste time, and I toiled relentlessly. In late April, it was ready, but I knew that sending it to the publishing house was not enough. I knew this book was going to surprise a lot of people, and I had to prepare accordingly for my life becoming as public as the book was going to be. I returned to Montreal on May 17th, just before my birthday. I brought it to Morin to be edited one last time. I went back to dancing for a few days in Montreal to support a few needs that were more urgent than others, such as being able to buy enough products to start my own hair salon in Vancouver. Finally, before leaving Montreal, I contacted Sylvano, but oddly, he didn't want to see me.

Dispirited, I joined Mr. Morin to make some changes to a few parts of Precious. It was essential that I promote my first book. I wanted to appear on two shows on Radio Canada, so I wrote them the following letter:

*"Dear Sir or Madam:*

*Today I thank God to see this day, a day that I many times never thought I would witness but so often hoped and wished for. This morning I woke up, and it was done. A second publisher in Paris has just accepted my work. It took me 30 minutes to realize that I had reached another level. I remember that two years ago, when I had just finished The Legend of the Sisters Soul,*

*I still had no experience and no one to advise me. I sent my book to a dozen publishers in Montreal, and all of them turned me down.*

*Some of them didn't even provide an explanation. Only one advised me to do a better job of revising my work. I thank her sincerely for not having completely ignored me. I nevertheless continued all my efforts until my manuscript was almost perfect. After two and a half years of working without being discouraged, I finally reached the point where I realized that's it. I did it. It's a story that will go down in history as a classic. I know it. I had felt it.*

*On June 25th, I sent them my second book, which is now finished, and I can guarantee you that it is not to be taken lightly. The two books were written at the same time. The second is entitled My Precious and is about World War III. How can I explain to you what I knew about the elections in the United States two and a half years ago without seeming crazy? Yet I wrote it, a book about what was going to happen and who would win the election.*

*I knew it before it even happened. I didn't stop telling my friends and others that I had started a book and that I was going to sign a book contract, yet no one believed me. I grew up in Haiti, and my situation was never easy. I promised myself for that reason that someday I would be a source of blessings for those who are in need like I was. I only wish that, whoever you are, you give me a chance to promote my fantasy novel on your show. I will come with a few copies if ever I am to appear. I can guarantee you that you will not regret it. I currently live in Vancouver, but I would be overjoyed to return to Montreal, the city where most of my family, friends and acquaintances live. I leave it to you to look into my contract, and I take this occasion to thank you for the decision that you will make for the best of all of us.*

*May God bless you . . .*
*Kind regards,*
*Melissa Joane Châtel*

I waited for their answer, knowing deep in my heart that it would eventually happen. On June 25th, I was finally ready to send My Precious for the first time to my publisher. Two weeks later, on July 9th, 2017, I signed a book contract for my life story with Éditions Vérone, an entirely new story which was a mystery to everyone. There were some rather obvious items in certain parts of Precious that raised the public's interest. More than anything, I wanted to provide an explanation to the man I was going to marry soon.

"One day you came into my life and that day, I no longer wanted you to leave. You come, and you go, each time leaving me with tremendous doubts and heartbreak. However, when you come back, I'll take you back as if nothing had ever happened. When I wanted to return to Montreal to promote The Legend, you made a place for me in your home for the first time. I was hoping that there would also be a place in your heart, but it required a lot of patience to get there. You came to see me more than once in Vancouver, and my only desire was to be yours like I would have never thought I would belong to anyone. You wanted to make the decision alone, and we both know how things ended between us. I waited for three years to give you a chance to do something else with your life. Despite what we've been through, and because things will never again become what they were, I know that you'll always be my true love."

It was as if our meeting was written in the sky for thousands of years and Sylvano felt it even before the book had made its way in the world. Our story was not only made up of sad moments. For a time, he became an extraordinary companion who supported my every little whim. We lived our love story to the fullest! Then, there were too many disagreements between us. We were two extreme individuals, and it is for this reason that we didn't know how to deal with all that glory.

All the exaggerated parts of this book are just the fruits of an oversized imagination that I wanted to develop, but if I had the power to control my feelings when I'm in the presence of someone, I would not have hesitated a single second to become his wife. I would have liked to never change partners, but life goes in unexpected ways that we only understand later. One day we suffer. Another day, we live as though yesterday never existed. Often, I wonder if there are things that will really happen by writing this book. I had planned my future marriage to Jack almost three years ago, but despite this, I wanted Sylvano at all costs. My question was always the same: Was it because of me that what I wished for never happened?

If this is the case, this part, I'm writing it for you Jack, so that you understand how my life has been a living hell. I wish I had parents who pushed me toward my dreams, but I did it alone. As for the bad parts, I am not proud of them, but they are forever part of me. They are me, and I can't do anything to erase them. I would have liked to become the new, long-awaited person in your life like I waited for you in mine. I hope that when I am finally before you, all my problems will be nothing but a distant memory and that together we will become one and the same soul forever, my darling.

I remember that on Wednesday, June 21st, 2017, I had returned to Vancouver barely two days beforehand. On Richards Street, leaning against the counter of my apartment, I wrote the missing parts of My Precious before sending it in. I was thinking about the passport I had received the previous day from the government. I had often dreamed of going on vacation but for a long time, life had decided otherwise. I thought about the foolish things I would have done, but for some reason, which is beyond my understanding until today, I remained imprisoned for nine long years in Montreal; I now know that it was for my own good. I had recently become a writer. I was getting ready to take my first trip, and it was for something of great importance in my eyes. I was afraid for a thousand reasons, but the faith I held on to concerning what I was experiencing and what was still to come made me believe that everything always happens for a reason.

Vancouver is one of the cities in Canada that I will never forget. I didn't have a lot of friends, but those I found were definitely worth the detour. I had to return to one of the biggest strip clubs in the city to meet another one of my best friends, Cynthia Czucz. Her dying mother asked me to watch over her daughter. It was a weird feeling since it was the first time she saw me in her life. I can imagine what she must have felt when she met me.

I really loved that girl a lot. I had the impression that she had found a sister, someone reliable who would guide her to a better life. I wrote her story a few years later. It was somewhat unusual, but I loved working with her. One day while I was watching her, I wanted to know what she was passionate about in life apart from the club and helping her mother. She dreamed of becoming a supermodel. She was a very beautiful girl who just needed a little help. I wouldn't say it's because of me, but I did contribute to her dream at the beginning of her career.

It was the same for Zak Santiago, who was a public figure in Vancouver for years in cinema but who never thought he would break through in the United States. He became great. Zak became a star. He shone like a star, and we worked together on a few films that I wrote. Because, after all that, I specialized in writing futuristic portraits for a few people who were worthwhile. Vérone became one of the biggest publishers in the world, and we've gone very far together.

In September 2017, I would have liked to appear on Radio Canada on the programs "Tout le monde en Parle" and "Plus on est de fou plus on rit." Unfortunately, when I made my request by letter, I was not yet popular enough for TV. I had to wait another year to reach that stage. Meanwhile, all the changes that had occurred since the beginning of the year had partly opened my eyes, because today I look at life differently. Things happen whatever we do, whether it's giving birth to children, which is the basis of all things, or bringing nations to war and destruction. We are the ones who hold the key, and no one can steal it from us without our consent. For this reason, I unreservedly apologize to people who come off badly in my story. I just told my version of things.

Today, my relationship with his people has changed radically, and each of them is part of this big family that I've never had, but I now have in my life and who I would give my life up for.

I remember that in July 2016, when I received my SACO Hair diploma, one of the most famous schools in Montreal, I did not yet know the importance of this document until I opened my many hair schools, MJCat International Hairschool, four years later around the world.

By the way, I would again like to thank my former teacher, Xavier Lee who, besides teaching me the best technique, also allowed me to use his beautiful salon in downtown Montreal on November 4th, 2017, for the first signing in Canada of my book entitled

The Legend of the Soul Sisters. The place was set up for happy hour with finger food and champagne; I organized a reception with my best friend, Mr. Lee and his mother, and a few members of my family. The conclusion of the extraordinary evening was filmed to prepare for the coming of Precious. The same thing happened when I had my classes at the VADA Studio School in downtown Vancouver. I must give some thanks to Mr. Symon, my dramatic arts teacher, who allowed me to become an outstanding producer. I had travelled all that way to understand the proper technique, and I realize only now that it was just the journey of my life lines.

CREATE YOUR SUCCESS

In late 2018, I brought my Precious to souls who had long been searching for deliverance. That same year, I didn't even use lawyers for my documents. You'll be surprised to hear that they came to deliver them to me in person.

God sent me the verse James 1:5, "If any of you lacks wisdom, you should ask God, who gives generously to all without finding fault, and it will be given to you." I knew I had a lot of qualities, but I was far from being wise. Sex work had long ago made me prideful, arrogant, disrespectful, careless, vindictive, and had conferred so many other defects on me. Nevertheless, I always loved taking care of those who were less fortunate with what little I had left. I gave very good advice thanks to my experiences, and despite everything, I held on to my smile and sense of humour. I had long been asking for wisdom, and when I received that verse on December 31st, 2014, at the Centre, it became my one great prayer. I felt that my success was happening very quickly, but I couldn't attain it without giving myself one hundred percent over to God. It was what he wanted from me. I was certain of it because in a very logical way, you should understand what my future situation would be: everyone would envy me for a million reasons, especially because I possessed a rare beauty and elegance without any extravagance in its form. I was about to become a very intelligent young woman as I progressively moved in the right direction. Above all, I would become a young celebrity who all women would look up to as a role model.

The media could easily have swallowed me up, and fame would have quickly gotten to my head. I would have brought God nothing of what he expected from me, and I was aware of this. He was counting on me, and I was becoming too proud for all sorts of reasons that pushed me to never want to disregard his divine protection.

That same year in 2018, my family was getting ready to reunite in an incredible way. I had not seen my mother, my big brother Jhonny and my little sister Jenny for seven years, and it just made me sick to feel separated from my roots. I spent everything I had earned over a long period, and I had helped my mother and sister obtain visas for the United States. The problem was that, despite all our efforts, we could never meet: they couldn't enter Canada, and I couldn't go see them for fear of not being able to come back. Most of the time, I was primarily concerned about my family and what to do to help them as best as possible. For this reason, the last two years, just before moving to Vancouver, I lived in a large apartment, and I had the youngest one come to my home every other weekend, not to mention the holidays. I didn't often see her, and I felt that the connection between us should have been stronger. At twenty-six years old, I realized that an entire family was my responsibility, and most of the time, it was sickening to me to imagine any change in my life whatsoever. I would gladly have given up that sad life. I would have jumped to trade places with anyone, but that wasn't so easily done. I spent most of my time praying. I cried the rest of the time, and my pages had become my only true friends.

With all that I experienced, I contributed to doing good. I dreamed for years of going to Paris, and I made the trip several times for some of the books contracts that I signed there and also in December 2018 with my little sisters. It was the first year in a long time that I had a renewed taste for life and celebrating Christmas. My family followed the same paths as I did, and I give thanks to God for all of these reasons. Two years after me, my great-nephew Michaël Châtel became one of the most famous soccer players in the world, and I am proud to have contributed to such a success. He was recently recruited by the United States, but when I had my break-through, it gave him an extraordinary chance to attain his greatest dream: playing for Real Madrid. I kept talking to him about God and one day, early in the year 2020, he followed my advice and became a Christian. I dreamed for some time, after a lecture given by Pastor Benny Hinn in Montreal, of going to Israel to experience the place where Jesus was born. I was able to live this dream in July 2020.

Just before marrying Jack, I went into outer space with NASA because I had been selected to be part of the voyage for having contributed to the advancement of one of their largest projects. I was nervous about the vari-ous changes that would occur in a very short time, and I wanted to have a chance to live elsewhere if things went wrong. I desperately wanted to be part of a future that I felt coming at an accelerated pace. I remember the words of Franck Nicolas, a great 21st-century author: there will come a time in our lives when we believe that everything is finished, but it will in fact only be the beginning of something. Each and every one of us becomes the master of our own destiny, but in reality, God is the basis of everything that lives on this Earth and even in the infinite. Everything revolves around him—we talk about it very little and act as if he didn't exist. The universe could not continue to evolve without his assent. We prefer to set him aside at certain times of our lives, but in the end, who is the one who is really losing out? Us or him?

We remain alive and move in very different directions, even if God gives us a chance to accomplish some extraordinary works to pass on to the coming generations, which is the only reason that proves that he truly exists in us through our good deeds.

The chosen one Dimitrova became a great scientist who participated in the space research in which I took part in January 2020. I believe our meeting was predestined because our friendship bloomed at first sight, and we had great chemistry the moment we began getting to know each other. He was an invaluable guide and had known for a long time what I was fighting for because he had read my Precious. He questioned me about what had pushed me to write such a book and how I could express all the details of what would happen in the future with so much certainty. I replied that God alone was the author of my book. He alone had sown knowledge in me that would change the vision of the world. That should absolutely be taken into consideration because he was the reason why I had become a great source of inspiration. He wanted to know if I really believed that he was the chosen one, and I simply replied that the answer came not from me but God, and that when the time came, he would know the truth and that this truth would set us all free. He was one of those men who dedicated themselves body and soul to their work. To hear him talk to me, he seemed like a just and profound man. There was no middle ground for him: He trusted He who for many years had always spared him any problems. He told me of his countless adventures, the orphanage that had taken him in, and the ability that had made him start to effortlessly surpass all the other children around him. He prayed to a god whose presence he felt when overcoming the many difficulties that he couldn't manage most of the time. He felt blessed the day when he was chosen among so many others to follow a greater destiny than just becoming a priest. He had been recruited from a young age to be one of the children who would replace their predecessors. He had long ago accepted his destiny when he began to hear voices. At first, he thought he was losing his mind, but soon he realized that the voices were no longer leaving him in peace. He then decided to understand the reasons for their sudden appearances. Quietly, he questioned them, being very careful to not seem crazy in other people's eyes. For years, these voices were preparing him to discover a world he thought he would never know. On his twentieth birthday, the orphanage hosted a scientist who was there for a one-night stay. Given his seniority and his trustworthiness, he was asked to bring food to the visitor. Led by an invisible force, he moved forward with the tray to the table when, suddenly, his eyes fell on some documents. He deciphered out loud, without realizing it, every message encoded on the pages. He wasn't aware of the surprise of the stranger behind him, who believed he had finally found a miracle after years of searching.

The American scientist, Allsort Sasada, was part of the Italian elite, having grown up in the United States where NASA had recruited him from an early age because of his skill in advanced sciences. For the first time in his life, this man was having the unique experience of discovering such a prodigy, who was able to understand years of research that he had only understood after an eternity. He asked him to sit down and wanted to know everything about him. That there was absolutely nothing to tell because he had spent his life in an orphanage was his only sad answer. He had never known his parents, and prayer had become his true and only confidant. After a long conversation, Allsort asked him not to talk to anyone about everything that they had learned about each other. He was leaving the next day to attend a meeting of the highest importance. He promised to come back soon and, when that day came, nothing would be as it was before. This very influential man spoke about Dimitrova to the most reliable people he knew to avoid endangering the young man's life. A month later, a car parked in front of the orphanage and took the young boy to the American bases built especially for cases of this kind. It was the first time that they were recruiting a case like Dimitrova, and it didn't take long to visit all the secret forces that had remained in the shadows until that day. They made him take countless tests that the young man passed with much more success than they had ever seen before. He received other information necessary for his development to become a good leader for his colleagues. He was surprised to see how lucky he was, but the reasons for his success remained unknown to him. He told me that he had stumbled upon my Precious among hundreds of books in a small antique shop in England and had ended up deciding to buy it to read on his own time. The tremendous shock he experienced reading the lines of such a book and seeing his life exposed therein without the author knowing him became the answer to all his questions. He confided in me that he had personally selected me to be part of the journey, understanding that it would be one of the few chances he would have to meet me. He had to see for himself that I was not a completely different person than the one described within the simple book of fiction. He was not disappointed to see that I was one of those who were in the same boat as he was. He seemed delighted to have made the best decision about me. He was disappointed to see my heart love another after I had disclosed the details of my personal situation, but he proved to be very respectful and did not make any improper gestures. We prayed together, and our two minds merged in a remarkable way. He asked me other questions that I couldn't answer about many topics. I asked him, despite his protests, to come participate in my prayers when he was ready and not before.

My trip lasted a month, and each passing day became a unique and different experience that made me further bless the greatness of God, who reigned in all that I undertook. I knew that the day would come when I would see Dimitrova again, and I very clearly made him understand that he had to position himself and do so quickly. He was still single, and I was very sorry that he knew nothing beyond his profession. I was afraid that by staying that way he would not succeed in being truly fulfilled. I had become aware that God had allowed me to make contact with a man of such high importance, because at the beginning, I can tell you frankly that Precious was the result of an overdeveloped imagination portraying a still distant and unreal future.

I thanked God every day for having put such tangible evidence on my path. I kept praying for Dimitrova after that meeting so that he too could be touched. I wanted him to become aware of what was soon about to happen, and I was frightened of it. I had set a date to get married a day after my birthday, May 19th, 2020, and in no time, this was known throughout the world. I had made the effort to send an invitation to the astronaut scientist, but I didn't expect him to be present because I knew of his incredibly busy schedule. The surprise I had in seeing him among my guests was the same as when Jack made his proposal. He had freed himself up and had responded to my invitation without any hesitation, he confessed to me when we finally had a moment to chat. He had fallen under the spell of my lovely little sister Jenny, and, from time to time, I saw that their gazes were increasing in intensity and insistence. I made the effort of playing matchmaker, singing the praises of one to the other. During the reception, once the discussion got going between them, they didn't let up for the entire evening. My little sisters had settled down just like I had by becoming servants of the Lord; I was not afraid that they would let themselves get carried away by a desire to engage in sexual pleasures during that type of event. My marriage, thank God, was a real success, and the next day I went to the Bahamas with the feeling that I had finally been able to have such a special day. I had been patient, and I was about to reap the benefits. Miraculously, a week later on the way back from my honeymoon, I learned that I was expecting a baby. Feeling great discomfort four months later, I decided to see my gynecologist. What a surprise it was to realize that instead of one child, I was carrying two completely healthy little girls. I couldn't believe that life was giving me the chance to bring life into the world after so many years of doubt and misery. Despite this happiness, I experienced the most painful pregnancy in the world. Three words describe what it was for me: a real nightmare. The twins were becoming increasingly unpleasant, and I was eager, after seven endlessly long months, to give birth. I spent most of the time weeping and begging God that I would reach the end of that calamity. I had become obese, and I couldn't feel my legs anymore in the last days before giving birth. Luckily, my mom and Jack's mother came to give me a helping hand whenever they had the chance. Finally, on February 2nd, 2021, I gave birth to two beautiful little girls who resembled each other like two peas in a pod. The only difference in their likeness, which could not have made it more difficult to differentiate between them, was the colour of their eyes. One had inherited Jack's blue eyes, and the other, blue-green eyes; I always felt a little twinge in my heart to know that neither one had inherited mine. Once freed from the weight, I resumed the many activities that I was beginning to miss. In a very short time, I had become a happy mother, wife, associate, the charitable aid worker with various organizations and, above all, the servant of the Lord. I hadn't realized all the changes that had occurred while I was bedridden because of my difficult pregnancy. A week after giving birth, my little sister Jenny announced her marriage to Dimitrova.

I was not in the least surprised since I had seen it on my wedding day. I was more than happy to have to take care of my little sister's wedding. Lindsay and Deb had married almost a year before me and were happily living with their husbands, who were also part of the Hollywood entertainment industry. This marriage would be the last one and would put an end to all our past suffering. Above all, it would open the door to a new chapter in our four lives that would forever be transformed in the eyes of the entire world, as I kept telling myself as the days went by.

My sister's wedding was as successful as mine, and I was proud that she finally found happiness by being as patient as I had often asked her to be. I prayed with her when her world fell apart whenever she compared herself to our happiness. I was proud of her because she had always admired me and listened when I asked her to make certain changes that were needed for her personal development. Sometimes, of the four of us, I compared her to Khloé Kardashian in 2017 when the world revolved around the Kardashian family.

My little family went on vacation in Cape Code that same year. A month later, we bought and moved into a dream house in early July 2021.

We recently started getting around in a small Cessna for the various projects and activities that my husband and I each had throughout the world. I had slowed down on the production of films that I saw no use for now that world affairs were going so badly. My book had raised questions because each part was coming to life and seemed real since my sister had gotten married. I was being harassed, and it was one of the reasons why I had gotten away to Cape Code, which was far away from it all. But still, most of the time, that didn't stop me called from being called to come on this or that show to talk about what had propelled me to write My Precious. I didn't have all the keys, and I asked God to help me answer all the questions.

When the revolution began after the departure of Price in July 2025, everyone had been calling me a sorceress for some time. I couldn't do much to defend myself against such remarks. My husband watched me become increasingly unhappy because of this change without being able to do anything about it. One evening, while we lay with the twins, we endured an attack that destroyed half our residence. From that moment, we knew things would worsen. Dimitrova called us and offered to house us. I didn't feel ready to give up my house so easily, and I quickly turned down the invitation. My husband was the only person who knew me well enough to know that I was in a living hell. The only time when I left my half-destroyed house was to go to prayer centres that I had never given up and were becoming my only source of light. I knew that the book was my greatest success, and I didn't want it to become my greatest misfortune after so many years. I couldn't fix everything by myself and asked God every day to show the way forward in my life, and the lives of my family and all the other desperate people across the world. I was imagining the seriousness of the situation, and I absolutely didn't want to put my children's lives in danger. For this reason, I agreed to join my sister Jenny for a while, knowing it was also what Jack wanted. The attacks hadn't stopped since April and were beginning to be felt in various countries. I agreed to give interviews to several television channels who were begging me to respond to their invitations, only because of the pleas of my husband, who was also being harassed. For some time, he was having difficulty managing all that intense pressure. I felt that the whole world had its eyes on me and was expecting me to be the solution to the conflict that I had predicted. I didn't give them the time to bombard me with questions, and I started issuing my own communications. I wanted the world to know that, when I wrote that book, I was propelled by the Holy Spirit, in my opinion, but according to other people, by a mystical energy.

At that time, I had the image of a poor immigrant who wanted to prove her awareness to all those around her in the face of the miserable life she led for six years. I didn't answer all the questions that I was asked because I just wasn't God. God had allowed me to write that book nine years earlier to warn the sons of man of the scourge that would devastate the world if they did not repent. Except that they were all too busy with their trifling personal problems. Money problems had taken God's place. I could not understand why a girl from one of the poorest countries in the world was selected to bear that truth. Except that I was one of those who were chosen because of their heart and their life journey, which were unlike those of other people. A few bons vivants producing great works could easily have thought about writing that one, but because of their lack of faith, life had given me a gift. I could have taken my own life more than once if I had found the opportunity, but because of God's plans, I never really had the courage to do it. What does not kill us inevitably makes us stronger and allows us to attain another perspective for the sole purpose of reaching the full potential of our destiny.

I need to talk to you about the beginnings; it's the first compensation that, according to God, is the most important of all. If you can understand that truth and the significance of tithes and offerings, we stand out from others at the same time. Why am I bothering to broach such a topic? To simply recount what I did that made me surpass many of the era's other writers. When I knew that my two books were about to be created, I went to the Centre the first Sunday of January, and I got a message that, according to me, seemed rather special, if not totally crazy, but that I absolutely had to harness it. I knew my book was going to earn, as the first fruit of my labours, what I evaluated at twenty, thirty, fifty or even a hundred thousand dollars, if I had luck on my side. That day, I promised God, repeating word for word my understanding of the message, that the day I would make this dream—one that seemed beyond impossible—into a reality, whenever it happened, I would leave him half of those first earnings. I was ready to do something that would demonstrate to God that I would rather fight for his cause than live not knowing what tomorrow would bring.

Believe it or not, the promise that I had made didn't fall on deaf ears, because it is God who lives in heaven. He made us all in his image by giving us all the riches of this world according to our hearts. He simply hopes that we will arrive at the right time to pull them out of the hands of the Devourer. I kept my promise. I signed The Legend of the Soul Sisters on March

13th, 2015, with one of the largest publishers in Paris. My first payment amounted to more than $1 million. I know that some would have changed their minds, would just have left a modest amount or would have kept all of it. For me, a promise was a promise, and I wanted God to know that silver and gold came after Him and that it would change absolutely nothing if I obtained all the wealth in the world. Once it was in my possession, I gave half to my Centre and a few other churches according to their needs. I didn't ask myself any questions about what tomorrow had in store for me because I knew that my deed would not pass unnoticed in the eyes of the creator. I didn't need anyone's approval because my faith was unshakeable.

Let me quote the Bible, Mark 16:18:

"And these signs will accompany those who believe: In my name they will drive out demons; they will speak in new tongues; they will pick up snakes with their hands; and when they drink deadly poison, it will not hurt them at all; they will place their hands on sick people, and they will get well."

And there were so many more miracles through faith. I can guarantee you that, two months after my insane act, my book, paid for by the Government of the Canada, would be translated into fifteen different languages and would become the best-known book in the world, which lets you imagine the sums that I was able to bring in afterward. It was only the beginning of what God had in store for me because I no longer walked alone, and I now had palpable evidence. When I think of my beginnings in writing, I had only one idea: to talk about my life, how I found it difficult most of the time, and especially how life can give everything to some individuals and nothing to others. I wanted to talk about my small, sad life, but I knew that I had accomplished nothing great and had nothing to tell. I then decided to write fiction as I unveiled my gift for the passion that is writing, but two and half years later, I noticed that some parts of My Precious actually described the future. In retrospect, I hope with all my heart that we will not have to experience the horrors of a world war. I would especially not want to frighten the people who will see this book as a kind of threat. This is just a book that has only embellished the horrors of my past. One day things will really change, and I sincerely hope that it will be for the good of all.

# CHAPTER 3

# *Autobiography*

AFTER THE MAIN POINTS of my earlier life, let me tell you the many moments that allowed me to change my point of view and see things differently today.

I was born in Haiti on May 18th, 1988. I knew none of my grandparents, but I'm sure when I was little, I wanted to have some. My father was one of those white men whose economic situation was significantly better than that of an ordinary citizen. Formerly, he was part of the Haitian elite until several unfortunate events caused him to fall to the lowest depths. Of course, I guess he didn't help his own cause by becoming a father of fourteen children with women who were much less well-off than he was. He was what we still call today a white Haitian, whose origins were directly rooted in the French colonization during the revolution. According to my history classes in school, these former French colonists never had very lovely backgrounds. Most of these men came from prisons or very poor backgrounds. As for the French women, the vast majority were prostitutes. That whole group was the bad seeds of a radically reformed French society that was deported to take possession of a tiny country, called "Ayiti" in Creole, the "land of high mountains." It was inhabited by the Taínos (from the Arawaks), a semi-sedentary, peaceful people when Christopher Columbus landed for the first time on an island that probably possessed several hundred thousand inhabitants. He lay anchor on December 5th, 1492, in the Bay of Saint-Nicolas, which would later be called Haiti, but it wasn't until his second trip in 1493 that he gave the land the name "Hispaniola" (little

Spain). He founded the first European city in the new world, called "Isabella." Primarily using trickery, after defeating the five leaders at the head of the country, the Spanish forced Indigenous people to perform the arduous work of gold mining. In less than twenty-five years, the Indigenous people were destroyed by the brutality of slavery and the diseases transmitted by the conquerors. To replace them, the new governor, Nicolás de Ovando, attempted to have Africans brought over starting in 1503. Most of them were from Dahomey, Guinea and Nigeria, which explains the Voodoo religion. The slave trade was authorized in 1517 by Charles V, who would revoke it fifteen years later, even before the Veritas Ipsa letter written by Paul III. Toward the end of the 18th century, the work of the slaves on the plantations strengthened exports throughout all countries.

According to the same history, I know that my father was one of the many descendants of the French colonists rejected by France. His name, Émile Châtel, always made me reflect a lot about my different origins. He lived with a great aunt after being abandoned by his own parents. Handsome and well-educated, he fell in love with the little maid who worked in their home. Around 1944, when my father came to adulthood, he categorically refused, despite the pleas of his siblings, to emigrate to the United States. At that time, he preferred to stay warm and sing the praises of Haiti. He was the only one among the few members of his family who did not emigrate elsewhere. He died in 2008 at the age of 83 in the same neighbourhood that had always been his. Initially, he became the biological father of four girls and four boys with the same young woman. As they grew older, things got complicated between them, and they separated, and each went their own way. In his fifties, when he was in a little store he owned, he met my mother. At the age of sixteen, she came to live in the same neighbourhood. She lived with a cousin who had done nothing but exploit her since childhood. She was six years old when her parents were murdered in front of their children over a small country house. Orphaned, she never had the chance to go to school. Her older cousin, who took her in some time later, wanted nothing from her but her willingness to do household chores in her home. A shy slender woman with a pretty face, she caught my father's attention. Shortly after, they became lovers. She subsequently turned into a good mother who did her best to raise the most complicated children on Earth. Finally, she changed her title to become the exemplary wife who he had never wanted to have before. The first of my parent's children died after six months with no apparent sign of illness. Then my big brother Jimmy, the joker, came into the world, followed by Jhonny, the black sheep and above all, the misunderstood member of the family; then me, the middle child and the most stubborn of all; my little sister Jenny, who has always been the least fortunate of the four sisters; Lindsay, who always told herself that she was none other than the wunderkind of us all, but who I had long named "the opportunist"; and to finish up this magnificent portrait, my little sister Deborah, the most protected and also rebellious, who was interested in Greek mythology. Later, Deborah would make me realize how much we looked like the seven gods of Olympus.

I was five years old when my father took a young boy into our home. We weren't rolling in money, but we had enough to eat, which was more than other people in our neighbourhood had. More intellectually advanced than we were, Willy quickly became my father's pet. As soon as he came into our family, he let himself be guided by his sexual desire whenever he laid his eyes on me. He wasted no time and began regularly touching me. I guess he couldn't resist my pretty, innocent eyes, which have always been one of my most beautiful physical gifts. At first, I didn't really know what he was doing to me because he had started gradually and always asked me not to tell anyone. I was only happy to have another big brother I'd share secrets with while growing up. Far from sharing the same feelings, he always managed to get into my father's head so that I would come home to him when there was no one at home. At first, he told me that I shouldn't spend time with the little boys in the neighbourhood to avoid mischievous games. Over the years, he changed his tactics to show how he wanted to help me with my math courses, a subject that I always had a lot of difficulties with. His classes more often than not ended in molestation when everyone was gone. I didn't understand his true intentions or the way he behaved most of the time. Very often, I wondered if I should make my mother aware of what he was making me endure, and then I ended up telling myself that the whole thing could end up being a real disaster. At first, I imagined all the torments that I would experience with the whole family, and I was thinking that my father would blame me because his favourite would no longer be part of our beautiful family. Willy blackmailed me when he felt that I was about to crack. Out of the whole household, he was the one who did best in most of the subjects at school. So, knowing my weaknesses, he always asked to help me with my homework. He took advantage of all the situations that left him free to pursue his very well-constructed plans. He had to be terribly afraid of what would happen if the people around me found out the truth.

Initially, he dared not make me lose my virginity, and most of the time, when he was trying to penetrate me, I felt a lot of pain.

I remember that one my mother's brothers, who lived with us for years when I was a child. My uncle Job very often brought me to school, and he was the only one willing to do it when no one else could. In this way, an indestructible bond was forged between us. Children at that age usually talk too much, but I didn't. Intrigued by my mysterious behaviour, he silently studied me. Years passed, and he had become quite an alcoholic without ever being able to change. To tell you frankly, he never caught us in action, but I know that his instinct was right about Willy's bad intentions. He repeated what Willy was making me endure whenever he was drunk, but no one paid attention to him. Sometimes, when I heard him reveal my reality, I wanted my family to end up realizing that he was speaking the truth. The more time passed, the less the truth could be revealed in broad daylight. Are you wondering when all this stopped? With time, by so often repeating that he would marry me one day, I had ended up imagining that he really loved me. I wanted to live a normal life, but the reality that I was experiencing didn't allow me to think that I was already living an abnormal life. Throughout primary school, I only attended convent schools. Would I have perhaps confided in a young boy my age if I would have been given the chance? As a child, I didn't ever have a lot of friends, and I only grew out of my solitary side in my late twenties. Furthermore, I felt a lot safer when my whole family was at home when I came home from school. Even if he had never admitted it to me, I knew that he feared my mother more than anything. Since I had become his favourite toy, he didn't attack my little sisters. I still don't know why, but when I was younger, I always pushed my little sister Jenny away; maybe at that time, I wanted her to undergo all the stress that I was enduring. However, I felt much more maternal toward Lindsay and Deb, who lived with us only a short time before leaving for Canada. Strangely, I forgot my sad moments when I played with Lindsay. She was born six years before Deborah. As a child, she made me smile, and I enjoyed talking to her for hours. I loved her, and I was protecting her much more than I did with Jenny.

Time was passing, and things were growing more and more difficult at home. There were eight of us living under the same roof. Despite my parents' arguments, which were sometimes about Willy, my father never had the courage to part with his protégé. In the second part of the story, I vaguely told you about my half-sister who adopted Lindsay and Deb. After years without showing any sign of life, she appeared when my mother gave birth to Lindsay. She fell under the spell of the little one and did everything to get into my father's good graces. She pressured him to let her adopt the child. She promised, especially to my mother, to tell my little sister the truth when she was old enough to understand. Four years later, with the adoption papers finalized, she left with the child. I remember having repeatedly told my mother that this woman would never tell her daughter the truth. I was not wrong because it was only eighteen years after their adoption that Jenny revealed the truth to them about their real identity. At home we never broached the subject until Deborah's birth. The truth was that, even if I didn't talk to anyone about how I felt, I couldn't erase the pain gnawing at my heart of knowing that I would grow up far from that adorable little girl who had become my ray of sunshine. I think that it is at that time that I started really praying. Deb's arrival helped me bear my still intense pain until I also learned of her departure to join Lindsay. Four years later, the same situation was happening again right before my very eyes. I saw the arrival of the woman who didn't understand the pain that she had caused me since she had taken Lindsay away. For the second time in my life, my heart broke into a thousand pieces. Driven by instinct, I often repeated to little Deborah how much I loved her and that she should never forget us. To avoid causing us too much grief, my parents agreed not to speak to us of Deb's departure until two months before she left, but even without being in the loop, I nevertheless felt it. The sadness in my mother's eyes eventually betrayed her. The day that my half-sister came looking for Deb, I saw Lindsay for the first time since her departure. She had become a stranger. She had been brainwashed that she only should speak to us if her new mother could control the conversation. To top it all off, she thought that all of us were her cousins.

Very quickly, their departure forced me to understand my family's reality. I was growing up and becoming very mature for my age. I understood that their departures did not change the fact that we did not have the means to meet everyone's needs in the household. I very seriously thought about how to escape from that painful reality and saw all the pressure that my mother was under because of us. Compared to the others, I was the only one who never demanded anything of my parents. I always thought two and even three times before doing anything that could jeopardize the family. In my time, to get into certain good convent schools, you had to excel in all subjects. I was one of those students who had to study a lot to pass exams. However, the grades required by the nuns far exceeded those of the other schools in the capital. Which wasn't a bad thing, but all that pressure was becoming more than my little brain could bear. Already, at home, I was going through all kinds of problems! Knowing that my adopted brother was abusing my innocence because he was helping me with my school work sapped all the desire within me to stay in that kind of school. That year, I didn't achieve the desired level for my last year of primary school. Listening to other students talking, I realized that the poor grades at that kind of institution would be considered excellent elsewhere. I begged my mother to enroll me in another school so that I would not be held back. She decided to follow my suggestion, and that year, I started the school year in the same school as my little sister Jenny. Thank God, I wasn't the only one to have that problem since I had to take summer courses to get into the next class.

That summer, I became friends with a girl my age who became my best friend. We spent every class together and really loved laughing and talking for hours on end without getting tired of each other. I dared not tell her what I was going through because I was much too ashamed and afraid of being rejected. Gabie was one of those girls who had everything in life. Doting grandparents, intellectual parents and big brothers who protected and did not abuse her. A big dog as a pet, a big house, all the friends she could want . . . The most handsome middle-class boys pursued her because she had a better environment than mine. She travelled every summer for three months and came back with many very stylish clothes. To sum it up, everything I had never experienced in my own life! I wasn't jealous, but sometimes, I wanted to be in her shoes for just one day. I admired her a lot because she loved me for who I was: simple, shy, and as rebellious as she was. I don't remember how many times I thanked God for putting her on my path. She was as pretty as I am; therefore, there was never any jealousy. Thanks to her, I was spending less and less time at home, and I was thrilled about it. She changed schools for the same reasons as I did, and we spent a wonderful year in competition. I knew about her plans for high school, and I knew that my parents couldn't afford to send me to the school that she was about to attend.

I was quite sad when the year ended, and the time to enter high school very quickly came. I thought that the time had come to ask one thing of my mother for all the years I had kept quiet. My greatest wish was to continue my classes with Gabie and be part of her world, which also meant meeting the children of the wealthy who she rubbed shoulders with every day. I made my request without waiting for her to decide for me and send me to a school that was not in line with my desires. I knew that my mother understood my desire to make progress and for this reason, she showed me more respect. I was much more intelligent than my brothers and sisters at the time. I understood how the adult world worked thanks to the great passion for reading that I had developed at a very young age. My two favourite writers have always been Danielle Steel and Barbara Taylor Bradford. I've read other authors without them grabbing my attention as much as those two. My mother forbade me to go out to play with the other children in the neighbourhood, and I had to occupy my own time. Most of the time, I spoke my native language, but I always tried to think in French, like in my books. I rarely talked about how I felt because I firmly believed that I was not born in the right place. When television and movies came into our home, I knew exactly where I needed to be in the future. How would I get there? That was an entirely different story. I was very proud to have presented the story to my mother well enough to get into Gabi's school and would have even celebrated this small victory with a bottle of champagne if I had possessed the means. A week later, my poor mother gathered all that she had saved and made me the happiest girl in history. I was asking for nothing more. My brothers and my sister Jenny were green with envy, but it was only a fair turn of affairs after the years of sacrifices that I had endured. I promised my mother to work very hard to make her proud of me. I told myself that I would surpass my mother's expectations, but once at the school, I forgot all my good resolutions. The classes seemed very complicated to me. Boys started pursuing me, and my relationship with Gabie began to deteriorate. In just a few months, my grades were catastrophic because Willy wasn't helping me anymore. I had categorically refused to be molested by threatening to reveal the truth to the whole world if he ever touched me again. I don't know if I would have had the courage. But the fact is that he believed that I was able to follow through on my threats. My mother blamed me for making her lose all her money, and on top of it all, I could no longer control my devastating 13-year-old adolescence. I lived in a continuous inner struggle. I didn't want to bring shame to anyone, but I no longer felt able to unjustly endure the insults.

What would I have given to have parents able to help me find effective ways to solve my math problems in complete safety? I ended up thinking I had to get out of the house. I remember having read a story by Barbara Taylor Bradford entitled A Woman of Substance. I saw that the young girl's life very much resembled mine and that she had succeeded in running away from her town at a very young age to immigrate to a big city. Over the years, she became one of the most influential women after World War I. Except that I had not yet realized that it was a book! Over a year ago, I had discovered the existence of the border between the Dominican Republic and my country, Haiti. I told myself that the moment had come for me to raise anchor. One day, instead of going to my usual classes, I simply decided to hitchhike to find someone able to take me across the border. Unfortunately, I don't think it was my lucky day because, instead of bringing me to the Dominican Republic, he decided to drive me to his home. He drugged me, and again that day, I was raped. He knew that he would eventually have problems if he kept me with him. He placed me with one of his friends, who must have been a lesbian because she was already imagining a fulfilling life with me. My family was extremely worried after two days without any news from me. They found me on the third day with this woman, who was ready to take the risk of bringing me to the Dominican Republic. I remember the panic I felt when I realized that I was going to another country. Too much had happened . . . How could I explain to my parents what that man had done to me because I wanted to run away from home? I found myself in the hospital with my legs spread apart for a bunch of tests. I had no choice but to admit the whole truth. I became aware of the seriousness of the situation by observing my whole family's downcast faces. I burst into tears without truly admitting that I was trying to get out of the country. The man left the country as soon as he knew that the police wanted to put him in jail.

I no longer wanted to leave home. I was too ashamed to have missed my chance and find myself back in the neighbourhood with all those pathetic people around me. The ill-reputed neighbourhood was giving me homicidal ideas. Years went by, and my father never decided to leave. He had grown up in that formerly peaceful area of Port-au-Prince. But I wasn't rejoicing like he did to spend my youth in such conditions of poverty. I absolutely needed to be educated if I wanted to reach my goal in life. For this, I had to go to school, and I was afraid that others already knew the truth about the drama that I had just experienced. Then, a week after the recent hiatus, I was back at school. I was surprised to have become the centre of everyone's attention in so little time. I took no pleasure in reliving the still-fresh story whenever I was asked about how the attacker had treated me. I was always polite, but sometimes I preferred to continue along on my way without paying any attention to them. My grades in school continued to fall while Gabie's only rose. Her parents must have warned her to keep her distance from me because upon my return, there was a chill between us. Even if I didn't encourage her in her exploits, because she wouldn't necessarily have listened to me anyway, I didn't discourage her either. She ended up having a crush on a young bad boy at school. I knew that certain aspects of their relationship were becoming increasingly serious, but I kept telling myself that it didn't concern me. The year was coming to an end, and if I didn't pass, I wouldn't be able to go on to the next grade or continue being friends with Gabie. Finding a solution at that time of the year would not be an easy task. I felt lost and abandoned. I had a strong attraction for a senior boy who thought I was too young. I still remember how I felt every time I laid my eyes on him. He had become a forbidden obsession. I was dying for him to take me seriously. I wondered why he didn't look at me like he did the others. I confessed to him what I felt, but he told me that my feelings would eventually fade with the years. At that time, if I had known that this was only the beginning of a long list of disappointments, I would have joined a religious order as I had always promised myself when I went to the convent school. The years that followed brought me nothing but immeasurable heartbreak that ended up turning me into a truly emotionless girl. It took some time, but I finally managed to get through that bad experience.

My grades were not good enough, but once again, thanks to summer school, I managed to move on to the next grade. I had no choice but to attend another school. I realized that, because of my stupidity, I had lost my old acquaintances, my best friend, a very good school and all the benefits that came with it, and I had earned my mother's contempt, the accusing looks of my brothers and sisters and entrance to another, uninteresting school. I understood pretty quickly that my mother wasn't going to take risks anymore to make me happy. After all the criticism from my two older brothers, she didn't want to have a favourite in the home anymore. From the very beginning of the new school year, I was already thinking about leaving for a better institution. I was hardly thriving in the new one. I had to rack my brain to find a solution. Attending an outstanding school obsessed me more than anything. If I had been given the choice, I think I would have asked another family to adopt me.

That year, I met a very good friend who has remained one to this day. She was three years older than I was. My big brother Jimmy sometimes brought her home during the week. She was one of those very beautiful Haitian women with a dark complexion that I had rarely come across.

Knowing my brother, I knew that the relationship would go nowhere. From the first day that I met her, I wanted to be her friend. When they split up, I stayed in contact with her. I had detected something in her eyes that I hid in mine. My social standing was much higher than hers when I compared my house with the place where she lived. By becoming her friend, I realized that there were beautiful girls like me who lived in worse conditions than I did. Except that you all know the nature of man's eternal dissatisfaction and nothing can change this strange aspect of ourselves other than God himself. I needed her because I just had to understand the way she drew men to her without seeming like a slut. Thank God, the first time that Cassie entered our home, her angelic appearance charmed my mother. I had another way of seeing her, and my intuition was never wrong. I liked the fact that she was dating my brother because that showed me she had good taste.

Did you know that the vast majority of young girls who grow up with a white father always look for an ideal man who very likely looks like their fathers! I will not hide that, unfortunately, this was also the case with me. Black boys didn't interest me as a teenager. I found them uninteresting. After my catastrophic experiences, I disdained them even more. I had specific ideas, and I didn't want to end my life with one of them. This narrow mindset allowed me to never date any of the men in my neighbourhood. I was growing up and becoming more and more beautiful. Very often, I was approached by men whose intentions were not always very honest. I was the only one of my mother's children who was the target of so much criticism. They always called me a racist. I was indifferent to the gossip about me since I lived in an entirely different world than they did. My father was getting too old, but I wanted to have a father to confide in. At times, a hatred for my parents was developing in my heart. I didn't understand why people with so little money had the chance to bring kids like me into the world. I never had Christmas presents under the tree. There had never been a fairy to give me childhood illusions. I was wise enough to know to never ask for birthday presents so that I wouldn't be disappointed. The only thing I asked God was to allow me to live in a country where the opposite sex would only be white and a place where the mentality would be very different from the one that the people who I knew possessed. I wanted him to help me build what I had never experienced in my youth. Gabie and I no longer crossed paths anymore due to our opposing life journeys. We talked on the phone and only rarely saw each other.

I was increasingly spending time with Cassie despite protests from my mother, who was beginning to glimpse the risks I was taking with her. Of course, she did not wish to see me get pregnant, but I couldn't explain to her that I knew the risks in the environment better than she did. I gave Cassie the confidence she lacked; she was unaware of her beauty. In return, she gave me all the information required to enter the adult world. Carnival was coming up, and we agreed on the fact that it was the best time for our plans to succeed. We had to get tickets to get on the best podiums for the party. Staying in the crowd was out of the question. That option was not part of our plans. The tickets were found more quickly than we had imagined. The big day arrived, and we were very excited to see how each detail of our plan was going to work out. It was as if the devil had participated in our secret meetings, especially as far as I was concerned. I lost no time in meeting a man, who pursued me during the three days of festivities and bought everything that I asked without complaining. I gave him a date after the third day so that we could talk. I dared not admit my age lest he disappear. I also didn't want to lie to him. Cassie didn't encourage me, but she didn't dissuade me either.

The day of the date, I went straight to the point. I didn't want to waste my time. I had seen him at the Carnival parties, and I hadn't concerned himself with what he actually looked like. He wasn't ugly, but he was far from the image that I had of a man of his social position. He seemed much more revolting. He began by bragging about everything he owned. I think it's one of the tactics that most often work to bring down the prey. I knew that this relationship would never become real because the age difference bordered on the surreal. I gave him my speech on the value of education and the situation that I was experiencing at home. I wanted to change schools, but my parents couldn't help me. He came from a very good family; like me, he understood the value of education, so he quickly approved of me. He agreed to take care of my needs if it contributed to my progress. I was surprised that he fell in love with me so fast. I didn't hide how young I was from him, and it didn't seem to upset him in the least to learn about it. On the contrary, he told himself that if he helped me out with my education, I would eventually become the wife he had never had. He was forty-one years old, and he looked fifty-eight. The life of debauchery he had led for many years hadn't done anything to rejuvenate him. He introduced himself to my family and let them know that he had very good intentions toward me. He swore to my mother that he loved me and only wanted what was best for me. I found the school of my dreams, and he gave me one envelope for the entire year. Of course, seeing the generosity of that gesture gave my mother ideas. I was overjoyed not be of age, because I think that she would eventually have married me to Henry.

I entered the new school, and I promised myself not to mess around with my studies. That year, I met another of my friends, who came from the Dominican Republic. Cara was growing very close with my little sister Jenny because they attended the same school. Nevertheless, I suspected that she was much more advanced. Jenny was still very young, and I had to protect her from friends under all kinds of bad influences. My eyes were beginning to open about quite a few things. When she met me, she quickly abandoned my sister to become my friend because of our similar age. As usual, my hunch about her was right. I was also happy about this new friendship and that I had been able to keep my sister away from the outside world that I was discovering. After a few months, she invited me to accompany her on a visit to her country for the long summer vacation. It was the first time I was getting out of Haiti; I was absolutely thrilled at that idea. I spoke about it to Henry, who had become more than a mere acquaintance. He said nothing but was not too happy about it either. He saw all my excitement when I was talking about it, so he wished me a good trip.

So, I went and discovered lots of things that made me want to stay forever. In so many aspects, the country did not resemble mine. The men were not quite real whites, but they seemed much worthier of my attention than those black men, who horrified me at the time. Ultimately, I knew that to make this important decision to stay, I had to at least reach adulthood. I kept these new plans in the back of my mind, and calmly continued the rest of my visits. The third day, we were wondering what we could do when Carra suggested that I accompany her to see an old woman. I did not like this turn of affairs, but my curiosity got the better of my reason. It was still very early, and I saw myself going on a whole new adventure. Arriving in the area, I was pleased to see that the old lady was nothing like all those filthy women who sell you dreams and leave you more dissatisfied than anything else. Instead, I discovered a fine old woman who lived in a simple, very mysterious little house. She politely invited me to be the first to sit before her, and she carefully drew the tarot cards. I didn't understand a word of what she was telling me, but I was delighted that my friend translated everything for me in full detail. Here's what she ended up telling me:

"You come from a very poor country, and you're very young. Life has not blessed you, but that will change in a short time. You share the life of a very rich man, but soon there will be a second one. The two will fight to have you, but you will choose the better of the two. You'll have to trust your instincts. Very soon, you will receive a large white car as a gift, and you will have more, many more of them. You have enough power over the man who will be essential to your future. When you come of age, you will leave your country to immigrate to a country even greater than those you know right now. I see really high buildings. You will continue down your path, and you'll find your way with difficulty. But, once you find your path, you will become extremely rich, intellectually and financially. On your journey, you will help many people who will be expecting your breakthrough. All I observe in the last card is the number of people who will work for you. You will become a very influential woman throughout the world."

She briefly paused, turned to face my friend, and spoke to her. I was very curious because she didn't want to repeat to me what the old lady had confided in her. I absolutely wanted to know it. I knew it was something else that was also about me, and I asked her in front of our host. Shyly, she confessed to me:

"She advised me to never lose contact with you because, in the future, you'll be very useful to me. She very mysteriously ended by saying to me that maybe I didn't believe it, but she wasn't dead yet, although she soon would be. But someday I would find out that she was far from crazy. I admit that I don't understand anything anymore, Mel."

All that was becoming much too insane. I never had experienced anything like it in my life. I didn't know if I should rejoice about what I knew or the other way around. Either way, that woman never left my thoughts. I only half believed her. I was thinking that only time would tell me if she had been right or wrong. My vacation ended with parties and joyfulness. Encouraged by my friend, I had tremendous fun in many ways without feeling guilty. After those dream weeks, I prepared to go home with a heavy heart. I introduced Carra to Cassie, and from one day to the next, we became a wonderful threesome. I only have very special memories about those girls. The only problem remaining was that I still didn't like Henry. He was becoming increasingly urgent about me coming to live with him. It was as if he felt a potential danger coming that would prevent him from achieving his ends. He said that I would eventually have his children, and I understood only too well what was coming. The girls and I had become like sisters since mine was too little for me to even think about revealing all my secrets to her. I was seventeen years old. Cassie completed high school and found a job with some Arab merchants. It was summer, and her boss required her presence for a promotional campaign for a brand-new beer in the country. She invited me to join her. The event took place in the parking lot of one of the many supermarkets that belonged to her boss's family, which was not too far from downtown. Remember, in the second part of My Precious, I told you about the ex who would allow me to get out of the country. That day, in the parking lot, I was about to meet him . . . The prediction of the old fortune teller mentioned this second man in my life. He was getting into his car with his grocery bags when our eyes met. He later confessed that he had not been prepared to feel such strong emotions for a teenager. Being shy, he left without talking to me. Before the car completely disappeared, he turned around one last time just to gaze at me. That moment released a magic energy that forever joined our two lives together. Today, I know that at that moment, our fates had been sealed.

After that day, I didn't go home to my parents' house. I stayed at Cassie's, who in turn slept over at the home of a lover who she was barely dating. The next day, I was starving, and I waited to go to lunch for hours. She didn't come to join me, so I decided to go by myself to a restaurant that wasn't too far away. I had been waiting for my meal for about 20 minutes when I saw the man from the parking lot appear. He walked by my table and sat at a nearby table. We exchanged looks of surprise at first, inwardly wondering about the reason for such a coincidence. Then my phone rang and broke the tension that was beginning to rise. I saw that he was dying to get closer, but not wanting to come across one of those Dominican prostitutes who walked the streets of the capital, he preferred to keep his distance. When I spoke on the phone in perfect French, his eyes widened. I think that the call put an end to any suspicions. He plucked up his courage and asked if he could talk to me. A shy, blue-eyed, well-dressed man with a beautiful mouth, he spoke with a thick Haitian accent. I thought to myself that he must be like my Dad. We got to know one another, and I was enjoying talking to him. A former Jehovah's witness, he was the most uptight man I knew. He seemed surprised at my last name because his father had already worked with my father's first cousin. He still remembered him and had very positive memories of him. He was surprised that I had not yet reached eighteen and congratulated me on the maturity with which I expressed myself.

I was about to finish my third year in the same school, and at the same time, I was disappointed to see it end in disaster. My studies were beginning to take a hit because I never stayed in one place, and I couldn't find time to study. For two years, with the departure of former president Aristide, we had transitioned to a form of occupation. In my entire life, I had never seen so many Canadians, French and Americans travelling the streets of the capital. These officers partied a lot, and I was invited to many events. When they landed in the country, I felt that the time had come to leave Henry. I wanted something more exciting. During examinations, I was caught cheating in social sciences, and the teacher tore up my test. I didn't have the right to retake it, and I failed for the year with a very low average. I didn't want to stay at that school. I couldn't stand seeing all my friends going on to the next grade without me. So, I went to enroll elsewhere. Instead of two, I had three years remaining to finish high school. With all the relationships that I had with foreigners from the United Nations, I only discouraged the man in the parking lot and his good intentions. He was too eagerly pursuing me, and you know the saying, "Treat them mean, keep them keen." He was sending tons of flower bouquets to the house, but I was not yet ready to have another one like Henry on my back. He didn't look like him physically at all, far from it, but to me, they were in the same boat. I could see what kind of controlling man he would become if I accepted to become his girlfriend. My mother swore by him and my father, who was growing increasingly ill, took a few minutes to tell me that he approved of that choice for me. It touched me enormously because he had simply stopped talking from one day to the next. It was as if he had gathered all his energy to tell me what he thought in just a few words that afternoon: "With him you'll be safe from everything, my dear."

After that, nothing more—he fell back into silence. It was my father's last wish that later raised my awareness about that choice. I wanted, one last time before his death, for him to be proud of his eldest young daughter. I saw what my family was expecting from me. I had to take care of them. I was horrified at the idea of becoming an adult overnight. I had recently turned eighteen, and since I had come back from the Dominican Republic, for the fifteenth time, I dreamed of only one thing: buying a little scooter. I couldn't tell anyone because, in my country, women didn't drive motorcycles in the streets. I had never learned to ride a bicycle, and I was eager to learn everything all at once. I gathered up all my savings because it was becoming the idea of the century. When I get an idea in my head, I can't sleep until I achieve my goals. I paid someone to give me lessons in the afternoon, and I began visiting places to park my secret project on weekends. Two weeks after an untold number of knee injuries, I found myself in the streets of Port-au-Prince on a beautiful little yellow scooter. I absolutely shocked everybody. My friend couldn't find the words to make me understand his way of thinking. I knew exactly what I wanted by acting that way. He had enough money to buy me as many cars as I wanted, but he was taking his time to do so. He wasn't too thrilled to see how I could live without him. He realized that with me, it would be all or nothing. It took three months of excessive craziness to hear him tell me that he was worried about me and wanted all that to change. He didn't beat around the bush just to silence the gossip. He left me one of his bigger cars to drive around. I had just gotten my driver's licence. The car's colours made me think again about the prediction of the old woman from the Dominican Republic. A big white car—the truth of her predictions was becoming obvious to me.

When I decided to take our relationship more seriously by following the old woman's advice, it was at that point that my friend decided to ease off. He told me that he would help me pay for the rest of my school year, but that from then on, he no longer wanted a relationship. I didn't realize until much later what he was already planning to ask me. He had never liked the trio that I formed with Cassie and Carra, and he thought that the right time had come to put an end to those friendships. Often in the past, when he requested my presence and didn't find me, most often it was because I was always with my two friends. He had very unfavourable opinions of the girls. To top it all off, I saw that the more he pushed me away, the more I wanted to bring him closer to me. I hadn't been rejected by a man in a long time. I couldn't believe my ears. He made his request without much delay so that I would change my mind. Of course, I assented, because I thought I would still see my friends without his knowledge. My friend was one of those men who could be as dumb as a doornail, so that didn't take any genius on my part. He was very pleased with my new effort to be submissive. That night after he was gone, I called my friends to let them know that there would be a slight change in our relations. I explained the situation, and they ended up saying that I was right.

I wasn't seeing them very much because I was resuming a busy new school year. Between my school work and my new relationship, I was overwhelmed. At the beginning of that relationship, I had accepted the idea of settling down for the first time to get accustomed to the new boring life that awaited me. As the days passed, my good resolutions ended up falling by the wayside. I had grown much too used to the money. I didn't know how to belong to one man to satisfy all my whims. I had become greedy because I always wanted to have more than I was getting. Having little choice, and due to being monitored all the time, I ended up calming down a bit. Whenever a dispute arose between us, I let all my desire to rebel regain control of my thoughts. That relationship was the worst of all my relationships. I successfully completed my school year, and toward the end of the summer, Cassie called me to tell me of her decision to move to the Dominican Republic. I already knew what my friend's answer would be if I asked him if I could spend the holidays with Cassie. So, I thought it would be a good idea to start a fight between us. I took advantage of the fact that we weren't speaking to each other for a few days to get on the first bus to Cabarete. He lost his mind in anger when he didn't have any news from me. He moved heaven and earth to find my address there. I was living such a life of debauchery that I had decided not to go back home anymore. My only problem was to find a job so that I could continue to live without worries. Cassie wasn't living in better conditions than I was, but she had found a Canadian who sent her a little money from time to time. One night, I came across a young American policeman who was not uninteresting to me. Twice, he flew to come and see me, and I was really starting to like him. My friend sent me more than one person to reason with me and get me to go back on my decision of not wanting to go home. I wanted to continue my life in Cabarete until I would eventually marry a foreigner who wouldn't know anything about my past. Thank God, he used another tactic: sending me one of my half-sisters, who didn't leave me any choice but to go to Port-Port-au-Prince with her. I didn't know all my half-brothers and sisters, but I met this one around the age of fourteen. To tell you frankly, she always scared me more than my own mother. For that reason, when I saw her in front of the door of the small apartment where I lived, I didn't talk too much about my desire to stay! After three months of a sleepless life, I returned home without knowing too much what to expect once I would be back. I followed all the advice I could. I knew all too well how the rest of my sad story would go. I would never again see my handsome American officer because I knew his point of view regarding the insecurity that prevented tourists from entering the country without risking their lives. I was more than certain that by going back there, I would inevitably get back together with my friend. In any case, my family wouldn't let me do anything else. I resigned myself to enduring all the pressure from my family.

I had to start my last school year late this time. Despite my friend's misgivings, I had fought to get into one of the most popular schools in the capital. I absolutely had to end my year as a champion. He took great pains to win me back; I used my leverage over him to achieve victory. He gave way once again and offered me a beautiful CR-V he had put in my name. He did everything not to lose me again. He soon asked my mother to allow me to come live with him. At first, I categorically refused. When my mother told me that she would kick me out of the house, she didn't give me any other choice but to accept the ultimatum to go live with this son-in-law, who, according to her, would very quickly become my husband. I hated my entire family for what she made me endure. In sadness that day, I folded my clothes. Jenny was looking at me, and she didn't really seem to understand why I was crying. She must have imagined that it was only one of my whims. In response, I held her tight in my arms, wishing with all my heart that she would never have to experience all that I had endured. I was just happy to still be in school and have contact with people my age. With my Henry, I had gained all the attributes to fully satisfy the sexual desire of an older man. After all that I had put him through, I was questioning even the reason for his obsession of wanting to keep me. I knew he loved me, but I didn't have what it took to be able to fully share his life.

In my new school, I had become the most popular girl. I was beginning to shine in my history, French, social sciences and other classes. Teachers always considered me a valuable member of the class. In my eighteen years, I had never had such success. I was still isolated, and I owned the biggest car in the school. Everybody wanted to be my friend, but I knew that I wasn't there to make friends. But I had to find myself in the same class as the hottest guy in the whole school! I found myself with him for group work. Very handsome, tall, funny, white, long-haired, he was a rock and roll fan. I couldn't imagine myself being more miserable in my life when I laid my eyes on that boy during each of my classes. We exchanged long looks without talking about what we thought about each other. I was not available, and I was wondering about his real tastes in women. One of his younger cousins went to our school, and she liked me a lot. With her, everything became so much easier when I talked about what I was starting to feel for that boy. I tried to push my natural inclinations away, but they always ended up returning. I had everything I had always dreamed of, but the joy just wasn't there; when I thought about how I had obtained all those things, I didn't derive any pleasure from them. God, I couldn't stop weeping every morning as I thought about how my life would be nothing but pain and misery. For the last time, just before my departure, I came across a young man who would become very special to me. As usual that morning, tears were streaming from my eyes. I was driving to arrive on time before the school gates closed when our eyes met. I was waiting at a red light while he was at the wheel of a company car company going in the opposite direction. He only lived for three months in Haiti with one of his big sisters. Without seeming the least in the world shocked about the image that I was presenting, he smiled at me, gesturing for me to wipe away my tears. I wasn't expecting such a sign of attention, and I replied by smiling through my tears. Two months after that little incident, I ended up forgetting that I had come across a handsome man. A woman came to the school that week to explain to us the opportunity that some institutions like mine had to help students of all kinds go to Canada for their studies. I asked her my burning questions and jotted down her contact info. I spoke of this meeting to my friend, and I was already dreading his refusal. Nevertheless, I held on to the hope of making him change his mind.

This new opportunity became the only chance to change the life where I felt myself dying a little every day. He was happy to tell me that he wouldn't let me go. I didn't let up, and we started arguing. He wasn't embarrassed to talk disrespectfully to me. I no longer had the strength to hear him call me all the most absurd names in the world. You know now that I was far from being a saint, but I figured he had to accept me as I was since he had forced me to move in with him. After many endless disputes, I gathered up my few belongings and told him that I would be at my mother's house pending a better solution. I was thinking that I didn't have to endure a life as miserable as the one I found myself a prisoner in. Because of our diverging paths, I had eventually become very close to one of Gabie's young aunts over a year ago. She was thirty years old, but I had much more in common with her than my old friend. That same year, Gabie had moved to the United States, and I was starting to have gloomy thoughts about not being able to do the same. All I asked for was to have a normal life. But today I wonder, what is a normal life in reality? Her aunt invited me to join her group of friends to change my state of mind. I was seated with them when I saw the young man who had smiled at me the day when I was crying on the way to school.

Accompanied by his 12-year-old little niece, who he had to look after, he was very happy to meet me. As soon as he saw me, he sent her to give me his number. He was short but had a beautiful face. Half-white, half-black, he had finished his SSVD in Canada and had been fired by the government for misconduct. Instead of returning to his native country, he preferred to land in mine because his sister had lived there for years and was married to an upper-class Haitian. After the party, I didn't want to hear my mother lecture me, so I preferred to sleep at Dome's house (Gabie's aunt). She didn't prevent me from talking to my new friend, and I called him as soon as I had comfortably settled in. For two long hours, we had a lot of fun getting to know each other over the phone. As I was fighting to stay awake with my eyes half-closed, I wished him a good night's sleep.

I didn't feel ready to go back to my friend, who ceaselessly harassed me the next day. I was tired of lying all the time after several seemingly endless discussions with the new guy. I decided to tell him about my real situation. He didn't allow himself to be discouraged and continued to want to spend time with me. We went out together for a few nights, and I didn't care what people thought about me. I had managed to talk to my friend, and I told him that I no longer wished to continue with him. With his status in the country, and after all the money he had invested in the relationship, I don't think that he would have just accepted to let me leave right out from under his nose with someone else. He knew me well enough to know that I wouldn't change my mind. He gathered all the good people we had in common to ask for their advice. Some encouraged him to help me move forward by letting me study in Canada. On the other hand, I also imagine that others probably discouraged that idea. I think he made that decision to prove to me how much he still wanted to please me.

May God protect you, R. P.! May he be with you and keep you in everything you do! I will never be able to stop thinking that some people on this earth are actually angels in disguise. If I could have, I would have stayed with that man to protect him until his old age, but the heart has its reasons that even reason does not know. I grew up with a father who was too old to take care of me, and I vowed not to repeat the same mistakes as my mother. I wanted a young man who would play with and protect my children against all those people with bad intentions who exist throughout the world.

For two months, I no longer wanted to end the new relationship with my new friend. He must have been under a lot of pressure too because he asked me without hesitation to marry him. He was European and wanted just one thing: not to see me go. I weighed the pros and cons to make the best decision. Either I stayed in a country that horrified me and married a man I hardly knew, or I was going to discover a world that I had dreamed about my whole life. The time had come, and the decision was becoming much more difficult than I would have thought. My friend had signed all the papers for my departure. He was aware of my new connection with the young man, but simply preferred to be silent about it so that he could see me go very far away from him. Two days after having made my decision, I called him to ask forgiveness for not being able to marry him. I wanted to leave. I wanted to visit other countries. I wanted to be free. I wanted to see my little sisters again. I wanted to work without having to thank a man for what he could bring back to me. I was very young and even today I still am, but I know that I had opted for the right choice in deciding to spread my wings.

Now, more than anything, I think about that old woman every time I close my eyes and think that she was right about everything. At age 19, on November 8th, 2008, I departed for the unknown to make a new life without realizing that in reality, life is me. Life is us.

One day, you'll realize why you came into this world. Don't get discouraged, the greats of this world have been there too. When I began writing this book, I wanted to tell you about my complicated youth. I wanted to give hope to other young girls like me. I unfortunately did not have enough life experience, and as I was thinking about life and human nature, the idea of a different story combined with mine eventually came to me as if by magic. The story would be original, I thought to myself. Without a doubt, I was inspired by a supernatural force. Morin, my proofreader and a very good adviser, wanted to know why I wrote a book about a third world war. I had no explanation to give him. Two and a half years had passed since I had written this book. Everything I have written about the last election between Hillary Clinton and the President Trump has gone as predicted. In truth, I only want love, joy and life in this world. I'm sure that if Donald Trump is re-elected, a war will be imminent. We can all prevent this from happening if we all stick together. When I say "we," I mean all the nations that will be victims of the war. We believe that this is not our war, but I am telling you that there will be nothing left if it gets started, so act while there is still time.

Thanks to all of you who have allowed this book to become a real part of history.

Above all, don't forget one thing: God is alive. He is always faithful. He is the god of the past, of today, and tomorrow will be the proof of his greatness. I'm living proof of his good deeds.

Ask with faith, and he will give in abundance. Because in truth,

I tell you: everything I dreamed of in my whole life has happened, and Thank you . . .

MJCat

www.ingramcontent.com/pod-product-compliance
Lightning Source LLC
Chambersburg PA
CBHW070040030726
47506CB00003B/817